THE CITY
UNDER THE
BACK STEPS

by Evelyn Sibley Lampman

THE BOUNCES OF CYNTHIANN'

CAPTAIN APPLE'S GHOST

CRAZY CREEK

ELDER BROTHER

NAVAHO SISTER

ROCK HOUNDS

RUSTY'S SPACE SHIP

THE SHY STEGOSAURUS OF CRICKET CREEK

TREASURE MOUNTAIN

TREE WAGON

WITCH DOCTOR'S SON

THE CITY
UNDER THE
BACK STEPS

942780

by Evelyn Sibley Lampman

Illustrated by Honoré Valintcourt

Doubleday & Company, Inc.

Garden City, New York

THE CITY
UNDER THE
BACK STEPS

1

"CLACK, CLACK! Clackety clack clack!"

Craig came around the house being a space pilot, his imaginary ray gun dissolving unwary meteorites. But as he rounded the corner, the triumphant smile of accomplishment faded from his face, the last clack was swallowed before it came out, and he stuffed empty hands, no longer filled with glamorous outer-space equipment, into the pockets of his jeans. His cousin Jill was crouched on the sidewalk before the back steps.

"Why hello, Craig," said Jill politely. "Why were you making those funny noises?"

Craig ignored her question.

"What are you doing here?" he demanded suspiciously.

"Mother wanted to see Aunt Grace, and she made me come, too. Don't think I wanted to."

"Oh," grunted Craig in relief. So long as Jill hadn't come to see him on her own initiative, it was all right. He understood about mothers sometimes insisting that their children accompany them on calls to relatives. It was something you had to expect, something you had to go along with. If any of the guys happened to see Jill in his back yard, it would be easy enough to explain that her mother had made her come along. But if Jill had just come over to his house for no reason at all, that was something else again. He certainly didn't want her to think she could get away with that. She was a girl, even though she was his cousin, and the guys wouldn't understand that kind of visit at all.

"What are you looking at, anyway?" he asked a little more amiably, moving forward to see for himself.

"Ants. Aunt Grace gave me some cookies, and I dropped some crumbs here on the walk. Just look at all the ants come to carry them off."

"Huh," said Craig scornfully. "Ants are pests. I hate them." Deliberately he brought his foot down and stepped on one of the scurrying black insects.

"Craig Eaton!" scolded Jill angrily. "That was mean. Poor little ant. It never did anything to hurt you."

"Well, its friends have," objected Craig, sitting down on the back step. "They're always getting into food at picnics, and crawling all over you. Once they started coming in the kitchen, and Mother had to put out poison to get rid of them. And once I actually ate one."

"You ate an ant?"

"Oh, I didn't mean to," he assured her hurriedly. "It was his fault. I left half a candy bar on the front porch, and I didn't remember it until after dark. And then I went to get it, and I took a bite right away without looking."

"And there were ants on it? How'd they taste?" she added curiously.

"Sour. Horrible. I spit it out right away."

"Then you didn't really eat an ant," decided Jill. "You just bit into one."

"Serves him right for all the times they've bitten me," decided Craig grimly. He fumbled in his pocket for his new Boy Scout knife, opened it, and began whittling carefully on the edge of the step.

Jill watched him thoughtfully, but she didn't remind him that he shouldn't be whittling the steps as his other girl cousin, Georgia, would have done. Jill was a pretty good egg, even though she was a girl. He decided it was safe to confide in her a little.

"I'm going to be a space pilot when I grow up. Did you know that?"

"No. Why?" asked Jill curiously.

"Why? Why, because it's adventure. Who wants to stick around this dull old planet? There's nothing here. It's all boring."

"Do you want to live on the moon?"

"Certainly not. That's just a jumping-off place. I want to go where there's something exciting. Where there's strange kinds of people. They probably won't be people like we have on earth, either. I mean really strange ones, with maybe six legs instead of two, and maybe they'll have scales instead of skin, and they won't talk the way we do, either."

"Then how will you know what they're saying?"

"Oh, I'll learn to understand them. Maybe they'll have thought transference instead of words, and—"

"What's that?" demanded Jill, coming to sit beside him on the step.

Craig beamed on her approvingly. She was dumb, of course, but still smarter than most girls or she wouldn't be so interested. He gave up whittling, folding the knife and putting it back into his pocket.

"It's mind reading," he explained. "You wouldn't have to know a language to tell what somebody was thinking."

Jill considered the idea for a moment.

"Wouldn't you be scared?" she asked finally.

"Certainly not. As soon as they saw I didn't mean to hurt them, they wouldn't want to hurt me. We'd just find out about each other, that's all."

"Oh," said Jill. Apparently she wasn't as interested in other worlds as Craig had thought, for she got up and returned to inspect the progress made by the ants in transporting cookie crumbs.

After a moment, Craig got up and came over to watch also.

"They're sure dumb," he observed critically. "Or else they'd stop and break those big crumbs in two before they tried to carry them off. The crumbs are bigger than the ants, and they can't see around them to tell where they're going."

There were dozens of the tiny black insects, all coming or going. Those carrying sugary burdens in their mouths hurried as fast as they could toward a small gap under the bottom step. A second group, empty-jawed, emerged from the same opening, and converged by jerky spurts upon the little pile of crumbs.

"At first there was only one ant," explained Jill in a fascinated tone. "Then he went back and told his friends. They're probably laying in their winter supply of food."

"Ants can't talk," Craig reminded her in a superior way. "It's instinct."

Without warning, a new insect, a little larger than those on the walk, landed in the very center of activity, sending cookie crumbs and even an ant or two scattering in every direction. Although wings, like half furled sails, trailed from both sides, the insect must not have used them on this flight, for there had been no swooping descent. Instead it had seemed to fall straight downward from a cloudless sky. A moment later, a handful of other winged insects, somewhat resembling the first, littered the surrounding pavement.

"What are they? And where'd they come from?" demanded Jill in astonishment.

"Flying ants," guessed Craig, although he really had no more idea than she. He leaned over to inspect the nearest one more closely, and was gratified to see that it did resemble an ant with wings. It must have been stunned by the blow, for it lay almost motionless.

"It's dead. Or almost. Shall I step on it?"

"No," snapped Jill. "Why do you always want to be stepping on things, anyway? Leave it alone, poor thing."

The small black ants, disturbed at their task of conveying cookie crumbs from the walk to their nest, had momentarily left off work. Some had been startled into dropping the loads they were carrying, and the two who had been knocked aside were waving frantic legs in an effort to regain their footing. Now, as the children watched, those who still retained crumbs between their jaws put them down, and, as though in answer to an unspoken command, each advanced upon the feebly struggling intruder in the center.

"Now listen," protested Jill, anticipating a battle. "You can't all pick on him. It isn't his fault that he fell on your old cookie crumbs."

"Leave them alone," advised Craig. "He can always fly away if he doesn't like it."

"No, he can't. Look, one of his wings broke off when he fell. I'm going to move him out of the way!"

Just in the nick of time, Jill snatched the newcomer away from the onrushing ants.

"Poor little bug," she said sympathetically. "I'm going to take you home, and put you in a box and keep you till you're all well. I'll feed you crumbs every day, and—— Ouch!"

"What's the matter?" asked Craig in an interested tone.

Jill had dropped the insect suddenly, and now had her hand to her mouth.

"He bit me, the ugly, mean thing!"

"Bugs don't bite. They sting," corrected Craig superiorly. He bent over to pick up the discarded insect himself. "I wonder what kind of bug it is, anyway. If you don't want it, maybe I'll keep it myself."

A second later, he also flung the insect from him, for although he had been holding it between thumb and forefinger in a way he considered sure protection against the danger of stings, he had felt a sharp barb himself.

"Go ahead, ants," he invited angrily. "Eat him up. It'll serve him right."

But as he spoke it seemed that his voice grew smaller and smaller, and tinier and tinier. It had started out in the normal tone he generally used, but with each word it shrank a little until it ended with the faintest wisp of a whisper. At the same time Craig began to experience a shrinking feeling within his body. It was a strange feeling, as though he might be withering away, or else that everything around him was growing rapidly. It made him quite dizzy, so dizzy that he closed his eyes, and when he opened them again he couldn't recognize where he was.

On one side was a tall forest of lush green vegetation which grew so thickly that he could not see between the wide flat stalks. It stretched high above his head, as tall as the tallest trees, but unlike ordinary trees these had no brown trunks or branches, for the wide green growth sprang directly from the ground. On his other side was a white wall, made of wood, as high as the tops of the green forest, and underfoot was hard, rough gray rock which went on and on, seemingly forever.

At first he thought he was alone in this strange place, and then he saw that he was not. Advancing toward him, at a galloping run, were four of the most terrifying creatures he had ever seen. They were inky black, and their skins looked hard and glistening in the sunlight, as though they had been freshly oiled. Six legs, three on each side, carried them ahead at such a speed that even had Craig turned to run away, he could never have hoped to escape. A moment later they had reached him, whereupon they arranged themselves in a guarding position, one to stand directly in front, one behind, the other guarding each side.

Craig stood perfectly still, hoping the creatures wouldn't know how frightened he was. He made himself stare into the black face which was on a level with his own, and tried to look as though such an encounter happened every day. But of course it didn't. He had never seen such a face, outside of a nightmare or a Hallowe'en mask. And he wasn't asleep, and this wasn't Hallowe'en.

Three gigantic pearl-colored eyes stared unblinkingly back at him from the center of the creature's forehead, while two more eyes protruded slightly from the sides, in the places where men grow ears. There were no ears at all on this head, and no nose, either, but there was a mouth, which moved from side to side as well as up and down. When it did so, Craig had a glimpse of something that flickered like a tongue, and of something else that was sharp and might have been teeth. Protruding from the creature's head were two long black tubes with tiny holes in the end, and these tubes moved restlessly from side to side and up and down as though it was impossible for them to be still.

The head rested directly on the creature's body, with no neck at all, and the body itself seemed to be composed of two shining black balls, separated by a tiny stem or waist. The two legs in front were finished off with jagged edges, like the teeth of a comb, and they looked sharp and formidable.

Craig had never seen anything like this before. But in the back of his mind some memory stirred. Somewhere he had read, or heard about, such awesome beings. And then he knew.

"You're from outer space!" he cried. "That's what you are!"

A moment later he jumped and pulled back, but the creature behind was there holding him still, while the one facing him lightly placed one of the long black tubes on Craig's forehead.

"What are you?" said a voice in his ears, and Craig realized that the black, waving tendril was a speaking tube, an antenna, and that the creature was asking a question.

"I'm a boy. An earth boy," said Craig. He spoke loudly as one might address someone who was hard of hearing. "What planet are you from?"

"A boy?" Craig had the impression that the creature was displeased. "What a waste. Her Majesty will be disappointed. But perhaps, if she plans to keep you as a pet, the fact that you are a male and of no real use is not important."

The creature seemed to be studying him with its three milky white eyes, and when Craig glanced from left to right, those guards, too, were regarding him curiously from their many-faceted side eyes.

"Are you going to eat me?" he quavered.

"No," denied the creature mildly. "I've never encountered anything quite like you before. You might not be edible. Where do you live?"

"Why, I live right here in this house," began Craig, and then he stopped. There was no house, only a high white wooden wall on one side and an exotic waving forest of strange trunkless trees on the other. He had never been in this place before. He had never even seen pictures of anything resembling it. Where was he? How had he got here? And who were these ugly black creatures, as large as he, who walked on six legs and spoke and read thoughts through antennae on their glistening heads?

Craig knew the answer to some of the questions instantly. He had read enough space books so that there could be no doubt. He was on some far planet from the earth, and the four creatures were some of its inhabitants. The only question he couldn't answer was how he had got here. However it had happened, he didn't like it. He wasn't ready to explore outer space. Not yet. He gulped hard, for something which he couldn't swallow was sticking in his throat.

Perhaps the creature interpreted some of his confused and frightened feelings, for the words which came through the antennae and into Craig's brain suggested that they meant to be comforting.

"You will like it in our city. And today is an auspicious time to meet Her Majesty. It is her wedding day."

Craig nodded without speaking. He couldn't speak. If he tried to he would cry, and he didn't want to cry in front of these strangers from a distant planet. But he didn't want to be here. He wanted his mother and his father. He wanted his home, and he wanted the Earth.

"Come, let us march to the City," said the creature, and removing its antennae from Craig's forehead it whirled around to face the front.

Although Craig had distinctly heard the word "march," the pace set up by the four was distinctly a run, and encircled as he was, Craig had to run, too. Before he knew it, he was out of breath but when he lagged the guard behind pushed him on with a hard bullet-like head.

He had never run so fast in his life, and his legs grew weak and finally refused to go on. Panting with exhaustion, he fell down on the hard gray rock, and just lay there. If they wanted to take him to their queen they'd either have to slow down or carry him.

This time it was one of the other guards who put questioning antennae on his forehead, for the one in the lead did not immediately discover that the others had stopped, and was some distance ahead before becoming aware of this. When it did so, it turned and raced rapidly back to them.

"What is the matter?" asked the guard who had taken over the questioning. "Why have you stopped? Why did you lie down?"

"I'm tired," gasped Craig. "I can't run so fast."

"But it is a hot day," explained the guard in surprise. "On a hot day it is proper to march faster than on a cool day. That is one of the oldest rules."

"I never heard of any rule like that," protested Craig, but the creature was no longer listening. The first guard had returned and the four of them put their antennae together as though conferring with one another.

After a time they apparently reached a decision, and one of them approached Craig and placed the black tube on his forehead.

"It has been decided to carry you."

"I'm pretty heavy," objected Craig quickly. "You need all your legs for walking. I don't see how you and all your men together could carry me and still walk."

The antennae rapped sharply against his head.

"Must you be insulting? How dare you call us men?"

"I don't know what else to call you," explained Craig quickly.

"You see, on earth the inhabitants are called men. I don't know what you call yourselves here."

"We are women," insisted the creature, and the antennae against Craig's forehead throbbed with indignation. "We four happen to be soldiers, so you may call us Major."

"Women soldiers?" gasped Craig.

"You certainly couldn't expect to make a soldier from a male, could you? Silly, stupid weaklings!"

The black creature looked so terrifying at the moment, with her sharp teeth snapping in her powerful jaws, that Craig felt it was better not to argue the point. Instead he asked meekly,

"How do you four all happen to be majors? Where are the generals and the privates?"

"There are no privates in Her Majesty's army," explained the major. To Craig's relief, her antennae began to quiet down a little. "And no generals either. We are all majors. That way we do not have to obey any commands, other than those of Her Majesty, and we are all on an equal footing. It is more democratic that way. Do you understand?"

"Oh, yes," agreed Craig quickly, but he really didn't. It seemed to him that someone ought to be in command of an army.

"Very well. It's all agreed then. We will carry you to the City," decided the major.

Immediately the four soldiers grasped Craig in their jaws, two by the ankles, two by the shoulders. He felt himself being raised in the air, and a minute later twenty-four legs fell into step as they proceeded at a galloping run over the gray rock highway. Their teeth had looked hard and sharp when viewed from a distance, but Craig was relieved that none of the majors seemed inclined to close her jaws. He was held carefully, but securely, and borne along with as little bumping as might be expected.

They were traveling next to the white wall, and suddenly

they came to the end of it, whereupon the four majors made a smart turn to the right, and the road underfoot became very rough. Craig peered down as best he could and saw that they had left the gray highway and were now traveling up and down over brown, hilly earth. The lush green forest of trunkless trees was behind them, but here was a new kind of vegetation. This, too, was exotically tropical, growing to tremendous heights, but way up in the tops he could see splashes of brilliant color, which meant that these trees must be of a flowering variety. After a few moments the four majors gently placed Craig on the ground.

"We are at the City gates," one of them told him. "We think it would look better if you walked in yourself. But watch your steps. The causeway leading down is rather steep."

Craig nodded. He looked around for a gate to swing open, but there was none. There was only an opening with what appeared to be a white wooden timber across the top. Below the timber was a well defined road of hard pounded earth which disappeared into shadows.

Once more the four majors took up their original positions surrounding him, and again they hurried him forward into the cool darkness. At first Craig could see nothing at all, although his feet told him he was descending a steep, winding hill. Occasionally he had the impression that someone or something, doubtless another creature like the soldiers, passed them on its way up the hill, but no one spoke and the earthy cavern gave off no sound.

He remembered some of the science fiction books he had read. More than one author had guessed that life on other planets might be lived underground. Craig wished that he could tell them that their guesses had been right, but of course he couldn't. Perhaps he'd never be able to. He might never get back to Earth at all, but would just have to stay here forever.

Gradually he was becoming able to distinguish a little in the darkness, the gleam of pearly eyes, an occasional glittering flash which might have been given off by a hard polished body. He had thought that his eyes were growing accustomed to the dark, but now he knew differently. There was light ahead, filtered light, but light enough to see. A moment more, and they had reached the bottom of the passage.

Craig saw that they were in a large underground chamber. Although there were hundreds of black creatures, similar to the four soldiers, each rushing around at some task, the room was by no means crowded. It could have accommodated twice that number. Then he was aware of a most distinctive odor which seemed to hover in the air like incense. It was not an unpleasant odor. In fact it smelled more like vanilla than anything else he could think of, and he suddenly remembered that when he was being carried by the four majors he had received a whiff of the same scent. Here, however, it was very strong, and he decided it must be a perfume which they all wore.

As they stood there in the entrance way, one of the inhabitants bustled up to them. Delicately, she and one of the majors touched antennae, then she placed her other antenna on Craig's forehead.

"So this is the other new pet," she observed. "You have done well, Major."

"Thank you, My Lady," said the major gratefully.

"How are you, little girl?" asked My Lady.

"I'm afraid it's a boy, My Lady," apologized the major.

"Oh!" For a moment My Lady withdrew her antenna from Craig's forehead as though the touch had become distasteful. Then she put it back resolutely, as one who is determined to do her duty. "Well, whatever you are, come along. You may stand with the other new one until Her Majesty has time to grant you an audience."

Craig felt reluctant to leave the four majors who had brought him here. After all, one of them had come right out and admitted she had no intention of eating him. And while they had been firm about delivering him to the queen, they had not been unkind. They had been surprised to find that he was a boy, and insulted when he thought they themselves were men, but they had got over that. My Lady, on the other hand, gave him the impression that she wouldn't overlook his sex so easily. The touch of her antennae on his forehead had been almost cringing, as though she was afraid he might contaminate her.

"Can't I stay with you?" he begged the majors. "You can take me to see the queen."

"Oh, no," denied the major quickly. "Only My Lady in Waiting, and some of the nursemaids who attend her, are permitted in the royal chamber. Go with My Lady. It is proper."

My Lady's antennae quivered violently, but whether it was with pride or indignation Craig did not know. But he was sure that it would do no good to argue further, so he obediently turned to the lady in waiting, who began racing, at full speed, to the other side of the chamber. Obviously he was expected to follow.

It was a long way across the big room, and Craig could not possibly keep up, no matter how fast he ran. Several times My Lady had to stop and wait impatiently for him to catch up. Then she would race on a little farther before she stopped to wait once more.

They must have been half way to the opposite wall when Craig heard the first noise which had been made in the room since his arrival. It was a loud, scratchy sound, and echoed against the hard dirt walls.

"Crick, crick, crick!"

He stopped and looked around, but none of the others seemed to have heard it, or if they had they considered it so unimportant that they took no notice. Then he saw My Lady, waiting and tapping her antennae together impatiently, so he put the strange noise from his mind, and began running once more.

At last they reached the far wall, and Craig was so breathless that he could only stand wearily and pant. He felt My Lady's antennae touch his forehead gingerly.

"Stay here," she ordered. "With the other pets. You will be sent for."

Pets! What kind of pets were kept by these residents of outer space? He had been too exhausted to observe where he had been brought before, but now he looked up eagerly. Before him was a gigantic black thing, many times larger than any of his captors. It was bigger than an elephant, and its body, raised off the ground by six jointed legs, was covered with shiny black skin that looked as hard as shell. It had a round bullet head from which protruded two long whip-like antennae, and a wide mouth, filled with sharp teeth, which was gaping at the moment.

As Craig stared in horror at the fearful creature, who could have easily swallowed him down in one gulp, the two sides of its round body seemed to lift in air. They came together, as

wings, and Craig knew the origin of that strange noise he had heard before.

"Crick, crick, crick!"

Heard close at hand, it made little drops of perspiration appear on his forehead. And then, suddenly, from behind the horrible black giant appeared something else which made him forget everything else. It was his cousin Jill, advancing joyously to greet him.

"Craig!" she cried. "I'm so glad to see you. I thought I was all alone here in this ant hill. Cricket, this is my cousin Craig that I've been telling you about."

2

"How do you do, Cousin Craig," said Cricket. "It is nice to have someone else around to appreciate my music. The ants, poor things, have no ears."

"Cricket has ears, though," Jill told him eagerly. "And guess where they are! On his front legs. He's very nice. We've become quite good friends already."

"There's one thing about me," said Cricket, widening his mouth in what Craig was to learn was meant to be a smile, "I am a good judge of character. The moment I met Jill, and told her who I was, she requested me to play something. A true music lover! She had heard of my reputation, you see. Perhaps you would care for a selection, Cousin Craig?"

"Not right now, thank you," said Craig hastily. "I want to know what this is all about. What do you mean, ant hill? Aren't these space people?"

"Cousin Craig doesn't have your appreciation of music, Jill Dear," mourned Cricket. "How sad."

Jill reached high up and patted him on his face comfortingly.

"He's confused, Cricket. We must get him set right first. Then he'll love your music. I know he will."

"Very well," agreed Cricket promptly. "You are in the City Under the Back Steps, Cousin Craig. The black ant city, of course. Jill tells me that originally you were both Mashers——"

"Mashers?"

"That's what ants call people," explained Jill hastily. "You see, mostly all they ever see of people is a big foot coming down to mash them. Unless, of course, they're crawling up somebody's leg, and then they're generally brushed off and stepped on."

"But where are we? I mean where is the ant hill? On Mars, or Venus, or where? Ants just don't get as big as this on Earth."

"Some very nice soldiers—they were all majors in the ant army—brought me here," Jill told him. "And when I asked them how they got so big, they said they didn't. They said we'd got smaller, because we insulted their queen on her wedding day, and so she made it happen."

"You mean we're shrunk to the size of ants?"

"That's what they said. But they said she'd probably forgive us and change us back after she'd had time to think about it. They said she was very nervous right then, because we picked her up just as her subjects were coming to help her remove her wings. And so she made us change size so that we couldn't keep her subjects away from her, or step on them. And then she had us brought here because she was too busy to think of anything else to do with us right then."

"A wedding is always such a busy time," smiled Cricket. "So much to think of. But the important point is, you are now small enough to live in the City, and the ants have undoubtedly taken a fancy to you, as they have to me, and adopted you as a pet. It's very nice to be a pet, because you're fed and bathed

26

and combed. You won't have to do a thing. The ants will take care of you, and you can enjoy my music all day long."

"Ants!" repeated Craig. "I can't believe it."

But as he looked around at the hundreds of hurrying, energetic insects in the chamber, he knew it was so. They were ants all right. How could he have ever thought that he was on Mars or Venus or Jupiter, or if he had been on one of those planets and met one of these creatures how could he have mistaken it for something other than an ant? The whole confusion was due to size. The world looked very different when you were only a fraction of an inch long. But he knew that he would never get used to ants which were the same size as he, or more exactly to being himself the size of an ant.

He thought back to the moment when he had first found himself standing between the high white wall and the exotic green forest. Why, the forest of trunkless trees had to be the grassy lawn; the high fence the last board of the back step; the gray rocky highway the paved walk. It had seemed to him that he and the majors had traveled a long way, but it was only because his legs were now so very short. They couldn't have come any great distance at all. They must have entered through that dark hole where the ants were carrying cookie crumbs, and right now Craig was in an ant city under his own back steps!

"I was scared, too, at first," said Jill, regarding him anxiously. "It made me feel funny when I knew I was the size of an ant. But the majors who brought me here were all nice, and the lady in waiting is a dear, and as for this darling cricket——"

Here Cricket unfurled his forewings with an appreciative chirp, chirp, and waggled his snake-like antennae like two signal flags.

"So there's no reason at all to think that the queen, when we see her, won't be nice too, and change us right back," concluded Jill.

Craig looked a little doubtful. He hadn't found the ants quite so endearing.

"Aren't there any boys around here at all?" he asked Cricket. "Every time I say I——"

"Sh," warned Cricket hastily. "You'll do better if you forget that matter while you're here, and after a time perhaps they will, too. That's what I do. You see, I, myself, am a male, but I've been around so long that none of them remembers. Ants have memories, of course, but they have forgetters, too, which makes up for it."

"But they've got to have some males," persisted Craig. "Babies have to have mothers and fathers both, you know."

"So they do," agreed Cricket promptly. "I saw the fathers this morning. They went outside with the mothers, the queens. Oh, it was a great sight to see them all scamper through the Great Hall, their gauzy wings fairly twitching to take the air. It was sad, though, to know that the fathers would not return. This is their only day to live."

"Those other ants with wings," said Jill in an awed whisper. "The ones that didn't move after they fell. They must have been the fathers."

Cricket reached over, and with one of his long front legs, gently wiped away a tear that slid down her cheek.

"Don't lose your juices that way, Jill Dear," he begged. "Think of the dreadful things from which they were saved by dying so speedily. An ant lion, perhaps, or a wasp, or a Masher. It may have been kinder that way."

"But there were so many of the poor things," remembered Jill mournfully.

"There had to be," explained Cricket. "Each queen has several husbands."

"How many does she have?" asked Craig in a scandalized voice.

"How should I know?" said Cricket. "I'm not an ant, so it doesn't concern me."

"But you just said you saw them as they went by this morning. How many were there?"

"I have never been taught arithmetic," confessed Cricket, "so I can't be expected to count. It's the second time I've seen the departure of the queens on their marriage flight, since I've lived in the City for a year, but I couldn't count the last time either. All I know is that several princesses left today, so there must have been many princes. There is no set number of royal children. It varies from year to year, and from colony to colony."

"But you must have seen how many queens came back to the City?" persisted Craig stubbornly.

"Of course I did," said Cricket. "One. The young queen whose wrath you somehow incurred. It was very unusual that one returned at all. They seldom do. The other young queens went into the world to start new colonies of their own. They will lay their eggs, and care for their babies, until such time as the babies in turn are able to care for them. I have heard that the queens of some species are unable to feed their own babies, and therefore have to take workers with them on their marriage flights, but that is not true of our ants. Ours are quite capable. They go on their marriage flights alone."

"Didn't the old queen come back, too?" demanded Craig.

"What an idea!" scoffed Cricket. "Her elder Majesty didn't leave with the others this morning. Her marriage flight took place years and years ago. She is only married once, you know, although to several husbands. And it is quite binding, I assure you. She never leaves the City again during her lifetime."

"But if you already have one queen, why would you need another?" asked Jill gently. "What made one of the princesses come back at all?"

"Her elder Majesty is growing old," explained Cricket. "She

29

is seventeen years old. Think of that! Her eggs are producing mostly males these days, and to an ant, a male is of little use. One of these days, Her Majesty will die, and her subjects will give her a splendid funeral. But in the meantime, the City must have more workers, so one of the princesses returned home today. She will share the duty of laying eggs with her royal mother. The young queen was the one with whom you had your little encounter. I doubt, had she been starting her own city, that she would have had time to bother with you at all."

"Then I wish she had been starting her own city," declared Craig. "I don't like being this small, even for a little while."

For the first time he began to examine himself more closely. Except that everything was in miniature, he had not changed at all. He still had five fingers on each hand, tiny fingers with microscopic fingernails. His clothes, reduced in size to fit him, were the same—blue jeans, tennis shoes, and a tee-shirt. He felt in his pocket. There was the same Boy Scout knife he had been using on the back steps, only now it was a size to fit his small hand, as well as a soiled handkerchief and a package of gum.

He opened the gum, gave a piece to Jill, took one himself, and, after a second, offered one to Cricket.

"I don't know if crickets chew gum," he said doubtfully.

"I don't know, either," admitted Cricket. He popped the stick, paper and all, into his mouth, and after a moment or two, during which his powerful jaws worked vigorously, he pronounced, "Delicious!"

"You aren't supposed to swallow it, Cricket," cried Jill in alarm, but she had spoken too late.

"I am not an ant, Jill Dear," he reminded her. "I can swallow more than juices. You will find me the daring type, always willing to try something new."

Craig looked about the chamber, studying the ants more closely. At first he had thought they were running about aimlessly, pausing sometimes to talk with one another. Now he perceived that many of them were carrying something in their jaws. From an entrance in one of the walls scampered a long line of smallish ants, each with a glistening white object in her mouth. One after another, they crossed the room and disappeared into another entrance on the opposite side. Other ants must be transporting their loads outside, for they were climbing up the sloping ramp down which the soldiers had brought the children. At the doorway, each had to pass two ants who were obviously stationed there as sentinels, for none was allowed to pass without being touched by a guard's antennae. Craig wondered how his own party had got through without such an inspection, and decided that the major in the lead must have vouched for all of them.

As he watched, a couple of ants appeared down the ramp supporting a third who seemed ill, and almost unable to walk. Once the sentinels were assured that the three were residents of the City, two others from the Great Hall rushed forward to help bring in the sick member.

"That's Fizz," explained Cricket good-naturedly, observing the fascination with which Craig was watching this last group.

"Fizz? The sick one?"

"Oh, no. No, I've no idea who she is, poor girl. Just one of the workers who was hurt on the job. Fizz is the physician, the doctor, who will take care of her now she's brought in."

"What'll he do?" asked Jill.

"She, she," corrected Cricket quickly. "You must learn not to make that mistake around here. What she does will depend on what's wrong with the patient. If she's only broken a leg, Fizz will probably bite it off. That's not serious, you know. She can get along well enough with five. But if the poor thing's lost an antenna, Fizz will have to put her out of her misery. She'll be no good to herself or the City without her antennae."

31

"You mean—they'll kill her? Just because she's lost her antennae?"

"Oh, she'll have a proper burial in the City cemetery," Cricket assured Jill hastily. "But take her antennae away and she's as good as dead anyway. She can't find her way around. She can't signal to her friends. She can't smell anything, or even tell when there's danger in her path. And, of course, you know by this time that she couldn't understand what anyone else was communicating without her antennae."

"Oh, I hope the poor thing will be all right," cried Jill. "Do you think she will, Cricket?"

"It would seem so," decided Cricket. "Here come the nurses to wash her up, and medicate her wounds. Fizz is running away. The case was entirely too simple for her to bother with."

"Nurses, too," repeated Jill, greatly impressed. But Craig was no longer watching the little scene between the sick worker and the medical staff.

He had caught sight of a polished, trim little ant galloping straight in their direction. Although the residents of the ant city looked so much alike that it was difficult to tell them apart, he couldn't mistake this one. She halted directly in front of them, and placed one antenna on Jill's forehead, the second on Craig's.

"Her Majesty will receive you now," said My Lady haughtily. "Come, Jill. Come—boy!"

3

Jill and Craig followed the lady in waiting as fast as they could, threading their way through clusters of ants which filled the hall. Even those who weren't occupied with the task of transporting something from one place to another were not standing idle. Many of them were washing themselves, much in the same manner as a cat cleans his fur. Others were doing this service for friends, and now Craig could see one of the uses for the spiny edges on the two front legs. They were combs which the ants ran over their bodies, smoothing and patting and grooming until the hard black surface shone.

There wasn't much time to look around, however, not if they kept My Lady in sight. She had preceded them across the floor of the chamber, and when they finally arrived at the opposite wall they found her awaiting them impatiently.

"Why do you dawdle so?" she reproved. "We are now leaving the Great Hall, and you must stay close beside me. The tunnel is long and winding. You might get lost unless you are with me."

"We can't keep up with you, My Lady," panted Jill. "We have only two legs, and you have six."

"You have four," corrected My Lady instantly. "Why do you not use all four when you walk? It is true that you could not walk as fast with four as I with six, but you could walk twice as fast as you now do using only two."

"These are arms, not legs, and we aren't meant to walk on them," explained Craig. "You see, we're human beings, and men are——"

"That word again!" My Lady's antenna rapped hard against his head.

"What Craig means is that we've always walked on two legs. We were taught that way," said Jill quickly. "We'd have to learn to walk on four, and we'd be awkward and slower than ever while we were learning."

"That's right," said Craig. "It would be just the same as you trying to learn to walk on two legs. You probably couldn't even do it."

"Is that so?"

My Lady's antennae lifted scornfully. A moment later she raised herself, and on her two back legs delicately pirouetted before them.

"Awkward, am I?" she demanded angrily, replacing her antennae with a little flourish.

"Why, that was lovely," admired Jill. "It was a little dance, wasn't it? I'd no idea you could dance so beautifully, My Lady."

"Sometimes I wish that dancing and grace were accomplishments to be admired," admitted My Lady, and it seemed for a moment that she was no longer quite so haughty. "But of course I know they aren't. We must eat without being eaten, and take care of the babies. Those are the only things that count. Anything else is of no importance."

She seemed to have forgotten the beginning of the argument, for she tapped Jill gently and ordered, "Follow me. Her Majesty will be ready to receive you soon."

"You sure soft-soaped her," muttered Craig as they ran along the passageway.

"Sure, I did," agreed Jill promptly. "And it would be a lot better if you did, too, until we get out of here."

The passage was a tunnel, and on either side of it were the doorways of many rooms hollowed out of the earth. In order to keep within sight of My Lady there was no time to stop to see what the rooms contained, but from some of them they had an impression of activity within.

"I don't know why they always have to run," panted Craig. "Why can't they ever walk?"

But even had she been able to do so, Jill was too breathless to answer.

At last My Lady stopped at a doorway.

"This is the royal chamber, but Her Majesty is not quite ready for your audience," she told him. "We must wait. Here, stand to one side so you won't be in the way of the royal nursemaids as they leave."

As she spoke a black ant, holding a small white object in her mouth scurried past them and disappeared down the tunnel. A second later, another ant, carrying a similar burden, darted from the room to follow the first. My Lady had placed a foreleg firmly around each child to keep them out of the way, but by peering over the rough edges they could see into the room.

On the earth floor, a small procession moved slowly from left to right. It was headed by an ant considerably larger than the others. Contrary to the general custom, this ant was not running, but was proceeding at a more leisurely pace. As she walked, she occasionally dropped one of the round white objects, which the nursemaids had carried past them. These were snatched up by one of the dozen or more smaller ants making up the procession, who immediately carried it out of the door.

"What's going on?" demanded Craig. "What are they doing?"

"Her Majesty is laying eggs," My Lady's antennae vibrated with reverence. "The nannies are transporting them to the Royal Nursery. We must not interrupt."

"My, she's going to have lots of little princes and princesses, isn't she?" marvelled Jill. "If they all hatch, that is."

"These will not be princes and princesses," My Lady told her, "but workers. The queen is the mother of all of us. Only she lays the eggs from which we all come."

"How does she know these will be workers, not princesses?" demanded Jill in surprise.

"I cannot answer that question," admitted My Lady. "That is a royal secret."

"So she's the one who made us shrink up this way," said Craig bitterly. "Something's happened to her wings, and it serves her right. I'm glad she lost them."

"Her Majesty discards her wings willingly after her marriage flight," My Lady told him disapprovingly. "She doesn't need

36

them beyond that one time, for thereafter her eggs will remain fertile. She never flies again. But this is not the new queen, the one who punished you. This is the old queen, her mother."

"Is she going to change us back?"

My Lady declined to answer. She removed her antennae from the children's heads, and stood waiting to be noticed, her milk-white eyes filled with respect as they followed her sovereign.

After a while the queen stopped her slow progress across the floor. Obviously, for the time being, she had finished depositing eggs, and the few remaining nurses now rushed forward to administer to her. Some began to wash her hard black body, others to comb and smooth it, while one of them stood directly in front of the motionless queen, and it seemed to the watching children that their mouths touched. Jill patted My Lady to attract her attention.

"Are they kissing?" she whispered.

"No. Her Majesty is tired after her work. She is being refreshed with a drink of honeydew."

Craig stared as hard as he could, but he could see no cup or receptacle which might hold a refreshing drink. He wished that Jill would ask My Lady to explain what she meant. He didn't like to ask her himself, not in the presence of the queen from whom they were about to ask a favor, for no matter what he said to My Lady it seemed to be the wrong thing. But Jill didn't ask, and no one explained matters to him.

After a moment, the ant in front of the queen stepped aside and My Lady, signaling to the children to wait where they were, stepped forward. She bowed deeply, then she and the old queen touched antennae, conferring together.

"Why don't they hurry?" Craig asked Jill in an impatient tone. "I don't trust My Lady. For all we know she may be filling the queen with all kinds of stories about us."

"Sh!" said Jill quickly.

"It's all right," he assured her. "They can't hear unless they've got their antennae on you. Cricket said so."

Eventually My Lady bowed, and taking leave of the queen, hurried back to the children.

"Her Majesty is ready to receive you now. Remember your manners, if Mashers have such things. Bow when you are presented, and speak only when she asks you a question."

She led them forward, and they both managed a bow which My Lady must have considered acceptable, for she did not rap them chidingly on the head.

Nothing happened for several minutes. The queen stood silently studying them out of her three pearly eyes, and they, in turn, stared at her.

Close at hand she did not look so much larger than the other ants as she had appeared from a distance. It was only her abdomen which was much larger and was distended on every side so that it looked like a huge balloon. Despite the frenzied polishings of her ladies, her black skin seemed to be lacking in luster, and Craig remembered that she was supposed to be very old. Maybe that was the way ants showed their age; they lost some of their shiny color. Her face, like those of her subjects, was without expression of any kind, so he had no idea what kind of an impression they were making on the old queen, and she stood motionless for such a long time that he wondered if she had forgotten they were there. Perhaps the milky eyes were staring through, instead of at them.

Finally, however, she reached out and delicately placed a royal antenna on each of their heads.

"I have never seen a Masher before," she confessed. "I find you most extraordinary, as well as pitiful."

Since Jill seemed better able to get along with the insects than he, Craig had resolved to let her do the talking, but this was too much. No ant, queen or otherwise, was going to pity him!

"You don't need to waste pity on us," he began. "It's you ants who ought to be pitied."

My Lady, standing a respectful distance behind, moved close enough to kick him soundly on the shins for his impudence, but Her Majesty did not seem so upset.

"Really? Ordinarily, you have your huge, ponderous size in your favor, but reduced, as you are, you seem to me quite inferior. You have only four legs; we have six. You have two eyes; we have five. You have no antennae at all, poor things, so you must be always losing your way, and how you're able to communicate with one another or find food, I can't imagine. Besides, your skin doesn't look very durable. I doubt if it will hold up very long, and must be very poor protection. How many stomachs do you have?"

"Only one, Your Majesty," said Jill quickly, before Craig had time to answer.

"There, now. See!" The queen waggled her antennae sympathetically. "You can eat only for yourselves. You can't share your good food with your friends, and that makes for selfishness. Yes, now that I've seen you reduced to a proper size, it's quite plain that Mashers have only brute strength to fall back

39

on. And brute strength can be overcome by brains. Not in my time, perhaps, but in the time of my great-great-great-great-grandchildren. Ants will survive Mashers. There's no doubt about that."

"People have brains, too," cried Craig quickly. "People are smarter than ants. Lots smarter!"

"People?" fluttered the royal antennae uncertainly.

"People is the right name for what you call Mashers."

"Ah. Have they brains enough to change you back to the size you were before you incurred my royal daughter's disfavor?" asked the queen. She seemed more teasing than angry, and Craig had the unpleasant feeling that she was laughing at him.

"No, Your Majesty," said Jill, frowning at Craig in the hope of making him keep quiet. "Only Your Majesty can do that."

"Oh, you are wrong," the queen assured her. "It is my royal daughter, the new queen, who created this change in you. And so only she can do anything about changing you back again."

"Could we see her, please?"

"I'm afraid not," said the queen. "She is resting now after her marriage flight. And later she will be very busy laying many new eggs. She cannot be disturbed under any circumstances."

"But you saw us," insisted Craig. "And you were laying eggs."

"Not so many these days as I used to," sighed the queen. "True, no one has criticized, but I realize my end is near. That is why we have a new queen to help me. I will continue doing what I can, up to the hour of my death, but on my daughter depends the growth of the City. And the City is the only thing that is important."

"Not to us," began Craig, but stopped as My Lady kicked him again.

"Please, Your Majesty," pleaded Jill. "Something else is important to us. We want to be changed back, and go home."

"I've already explained that only Her Highness can make this transformation." It was evident that the queen was growing tired, for her antennae were beginning to tremble. "And if you go back to your former home the size you are now, the other Mashers won't recognize you. They'll annihilate you without even noticing it. But I do feel responsible, in a way, since it was my daughter who brought you here, so I shall permit you to remain. You shall be pets and stay with Cricket."

"I won't be a pet!" yelled Craig. "I won't!"

To his amazement, Her Majesty nodded approvingly.

"Well spoken," she declared. "These Mashers have some antlike qualities after all. Very well. My Lady, they shall be workers, both of them. Now take them away, and see to everything, for I am tired."

4

"You surprised me!" My Lady approvingly patted each child in turn. "Your desire to busy yourself with work was most commendable, even though I myself considered your manner of expression rude and unladylike."

Just in time Craig stopped himself from reminding her he was not a lady. So long as he must remain here, he would do well to adopt Cricket's policy and not mention his sex.

They had left the Royal Chamber and re-entered the long tunnel, and this time My Lady was not running ahead. Instead, as soon as they were clear of the doorway, she had stopped moving at all, except for her antennae which wriggled furiously in mid-air. The sensitive black rods moved from left to right and up and down, and finally she rubbed them together, as people sometimes rub their hands. Then, as though she might have been working out a plan which had come to a conclusion, she placed her antennae on the children's heads.

"Perhaps you would like to be nursemaids, and take care of

the babies," she suggested. "It is a great responsibility, but it is well supervised, so we generally start the youngest workers there."

"I love babies," agreed Jill instantly.

"Not me," objected Craig. "I'm no baby sitter. That's a girl's job."

"If you don't love babies, we certainly can't trust you with ours," decided My Lady instantly. "Perhaps you might do as an engineer, although you don't give the appearance of being very strong."

"I'm stronger than I look," insisted Craig indignantly. "I'm stronger than you, I bet."

My Lady tapped his head tolerantly.

"We'll let Digger decide. If she wants help on her project, you may start as an engineer. But you mustn't be a nuisance, and you'll have to carry your own load. Come along, both of you."

Now that her mind was made up, My Lady trotted ahead as fast as before. Often she was completely out of sight, for the tunnel, far from being straight, turned and dipped, but now they did not try so hard to keep up since they were no longer afraid of being lost. All they had to do was follow along to the end, and there would be the Great Hall, with the door leading to the outer world.

"I think we should have stayed together," said Jill in an anxious tone. "I don't like you working one place and me another."

"Don't worry," Craig assured her. "I won't be too far away. If you need me, just yell."

"I wasn't so worried about me needing you as I was that you'd need me," explained Jill frankly. "You don't seem to get along with ants very well."

"Why should I?" he demanded huffily. "The main thing is to get out of here, isn't it? And back home?"

"Yes," agreed Jill. "Only we've got to grow big first, remember."

My Lady was awaiting them around the next turn. She stood in the doorway of one of the many rooms they had previously passed by, and with her was a fat little ant who turned and regarded them intently from her three front eyes.

"This is the nursery," My Lady announced. "And this is Nannie, who will show you what to do. We've arrived just at feeding time, so don't keep her waiting. There's lots of work here, so you'll be very happy, Jill."

Jill stepped forward obediently.

"Goodbye, My Lady. Goodbye, Craig. And for goodness' sakes, be careful what you say."

"You're the one who'd better be careful," frowned Craig, but just the same it gave him a strange feeling to see his cousin disappear inside the room.

It wasn't right for him to leave her that way. After all, she was a girl, and needed his protection. And it might have been wiser had they stayed together. Of course, he couldn't be expected to serve as a nursemaid, and equally of course, Jill couldn't be an engineer. But there must be some job in the ant city which would have been acceptable to them both. He decided to keep his eyes open for such employment, then come back and get her when he found the right thing.

My Lady led him back to the Great Hall, where everything was very much as it had been when they left.

"Go over and stay with Cricket," she ordered. "Then I'll know where to look for you when I want you. There are several engineering projects in progress at the moment, and I must see which would be most suitable for you."

It was not difficult to see Cricket across the room, for his glistening body, so much larger than those of the ants, stood out like an ink smudge against the earthen walls. But walking at his usual pace, it took Craig some time to cross the floor, and for the first time he began to understand why the ants ran everywhere they went. If they walked, they would never get anything done.

Cricket saw him coming, and waved an enthusiastic antenna.

"So you're back! And just in time for supper, too. Another minute, and I'd have gobbled everything up. Please help yourself."

At Cricket's feet was a pile of white crumbs which somehow looked familiar. Craig bent and touched one tentatively. It was hard and dry, but there was no mistaking the fact that it had once been part of a cookie.

"I'm really not hungry," he told Cricket politely.

"Aren't you?" Cricket was pleased, and finished off the crumbs immediately. "You may be sorry later," he warned. "Those were extremely tasty, and it may be a while till the next meal."

"Mother makes good cookies," remembered Craig, and the thought made him feel lonesome and a little frightened. He wondered what his mother was doing right now. Had she missed him and Jill by this time? What would she do when they couldn't be found? He tried to put the disturbing thought from his mind, since there was nothing he could do about the situation at present, and managed to smile at Cricket a little woefully.

"At least they were good cookies when they were fresh," he said. "But they've got awfully dry now."

"Bless your heart, Cousin Craig, my food is always dry. I've become so accustomed to it that way that I wouldn't know how to manage a juicy bite!" Cricket's mouth widened as though he had said something clever. "You see, by the time I get it, it's husks. The ants have extracted all the juices for themselves."

"I wouldn't stand for that," cried Craig, aghast. "I wouldn't eat husks for anybody."

"But I like husks," confessed Cricket in surprise.

"Don't you ever get anything to drink?"

"Certainly," began Cricket, then stopped, his mouth falling open in astonishment.

When he had gathered in the last mouthful, he had missed one of the crumbs, and at that moment a tiny brown ant, considerably smaller than the residents of the City, had appeared from nowhere, snatched up the wee morsel, and darted back toward the wall. The whole thing had taken only a second, but a second was long enough for some of the other ants to catch sight of the intruder. Those who did immediately left off what they were doing and gave chase. With twitching antennae and their six legs fairly flying over the ground, they pursued her to the wall, where they halted in obvious disappointment. She had disappeared.

"What was that?" gasped Craig.

"A robber ant," Cricket told him. "Must have moved in next door. They're smaller than our ants, you see, and they make such tiny tunnels and holes that we can't follow them. They watch, and when they see a tasty morsel they leap out of their hole, snatch it up, and run back before they can be caught. This time, the joke was on the robber. She stole nothing but husk. But there'll be another time. You can be sure of that."

"Why don't they seal up the hole in the wall so she can't get out?" asked Craig sensibly.

"Oh, I imagine they will," said Cricket. "They'll have to do something. When robber ants move in, they'll steal you out of house and home. Hello, here comes My Lady again. I wonder what she has in mind."

My Lady flounced up to them, and immediately rapped Craig soundly on the head.

"Come, come," she ordered. "Digger can use all the help she can get. Hurry."

"So you have to work for your room and board," sighed Cricket sympathetically. "It's just too bad you don't have a talent for one of the arts. That way they'd let you be a pet." And as Craig hurried after My Lady, the sounds of Cricket's music followed them: "Crick, crick, crick!"

For the first time, Craig wondered what kind of engineering ants did. Of course it wouldn't be nearly so diversified a calling as it was with human beings. Ants wouldn't know about electricity or mechanics, which left three possibilities. Engineers built bridges and roads and buildings. And since he couldn't conceive of ants needing bridges, and they didn't live in buildings, they must be building a road.

My Lady had paused at the entrance which led to the tunnel, and at first Craig thought she must have stopped to communicate with some of her friends, for a large crowd of ants had collected at that spot. But as he came nearer, he saw that no one was communicating. The ants were arranged in two long lines, and the ones in front were busy attacking the hard dirt wall with their sharp front legs, kicking and gouging until small grains of soil were knocked loose. As soon as this happened, the ant picked up the dislodged earth and galloped swiftly away with it.

"What are they doing?" Craig asked My Lady in amazement.

My Lady flicked her antennae at him and scurried away, but his question was answered by an ant as large as one of the majors, who came and stood in front of him.

"I am Digger," announced the ant briefly. "We are widening this doorway, and you are to help us. Hurry, hurry. Get in line. There is work to be done."

"Now just a minute," protested Craig, but he was careful to keep his tone respectful. Digger had well developed jaws

47

and powerful, sinewy front legs. "Are you sure this is what I'm to do? I thought I was going to help the engineers."

"I just told you. I am Digger; therefore I am an engineer. All engineers are called Digger, just as all soldiers are Major and all physicians Fizz." There was impatience in the way the antennae vibrated against Craig's forehead. "Come, come. Don't waste time."

Craig nodded meekly and followed Digger to the end of the line of ants. There were so many workers that they had to wait their turns, but before long all the ants ahead had knocked loose a few grains of dirt, picked them up and darted away, and it was Craig and Digger's turn facing the wall.

Digger looked at Craig and waggled her antennae significantly. There was no need to waste words; it was simpler to show him how this was done. Much to Craig's amazement, the ant lifted herself, as My Lady had done, to her two hind feet, which brought her exactly to the height where the ant before had left off working. Digger's hard front legs came down forcefully, ripping and tearing the earth until a small fragment was knocked loose.

"Your turn," signaled Digger, and Craig realized that he was expected to repeat the performance.

But it was not so easy as it looked. He pounded the wall with all his might, and nothing gave. He tried kicking it, but the results were no better. His hands stung with the force of his blows, but the earth seemed to him as hard as cement and

48

quite as durable. Behind him, he could feel impatient antennae tickling his back. The next workers in line were urging him to hurry, to stop wasting time. In desperation, he tried scratching at the dirt with his fingernails. If he could only get it started. What he needed was a sharp point, something with which to make a weakening crack in the unyielding surface. His nails only rubbed harmlessly across the wall; they were too short to do any good.

Then, luckily, he remembered the Boy Scout knife in his pocket. He had it out in an instant, trying to ignore the antennae in his back, and concentrating on the knife and the wall before him. He sensed, rather than saw, for he refused to turn his head and meet those critical staring eyes, that Digger was still waiting beside him, ready at any moment to reject Craig's services as an engineer and relegate him to the nursery.

The knife did the job, although for one agonizing moment he was afraid the blade would break. The point dug into the hard surface, and he managed to turn it a little. Once it was started, the earth came away, and he was able to force loose a chunk of dirt about the size of his head. To his great relief it was no smaller than the clod which Digger had extracted.

He bent over to pick it up, and immediately the ants behind him pushed him on. It was evident that in their opinion Craig had wasted far too much time already; it was up to them to increase their own speed and make up for his slowness.

The dirt clod was heavier than he had expected it to be.

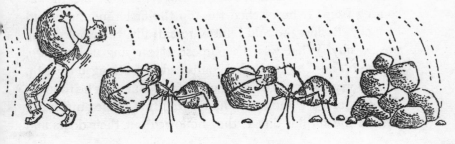

Clutching it firmly in his arms, he plowed his way through the lines of impatient engineers and hurried out into a clear space in the hall. Digger, her antennae jerking with irritation, was waiting for him. It must have been impossible for her to see ahead, for her frontal eyes were completely concealed by the dirt she held in her powerful jaws, but her antennae were free, and she sighted his arrival from one of the many-paned side eyes. Immediately she galloped off in the direction of the outside entrance, and Craig, clutching his own heavy burden, hurried after as fast as he could.

The sentinels at the door permitted him to pass, and he was soon climbing up the steep ramp. It was harder going up than it had been coming down, particularly with the heavy weight in his arms. Digger was long since out of sight, but it didn't matter, for Craig was continually being passed by other scurrying engineers, each grasping a dark load of soil. As soon as one went by, another caught up with him. For a second they toiled side by side, then the ant surged ahead, and there was another to take her place.

Panting and straining, he was suddenly aware that there were now two lines of passing ants. The line on his left was climbing, the one on his right was descending for a new load. It was not a comforting feeling, for he realized that the same thing would be expected of him. Once he had completed this task, he would have to return and go through it all over again, and he didn't see how he could. His legs were tired, his back and arms ached, and he didn't know where the next breath was coming from. If he reached the top the first time, he would be lucky. Besides, he told himself resentfully, the whole thing was so silly. What was the purpose of carrying dirt outside, anyway? The City itself was composed of nothing but earth. Why worry about a little more underfoot? But after he thought about it for a few moments, he realized that if the ants didn't remove the surplus dirt as they hollowed out their doors and tunnels, the rooms would fill up with it. There wouldn't be any City at all.

The sudden sunlight, as he finally trudged out from under the bottom board of the back steps, was so dazzling that he could hardly see. The sun, beating down on his head and shoulders, was like a hot whip, and he shrank back against its force. He hadn't realized until now how delightfully cool and pleasant it had been in the City Under the Back Steps.

An engineer pushed him indignantly out of the way, for he was blocking her path, and Craig trudged on. It didn't matter that the Digger ahead had disappeared from sight behind a tall brown hill, for there would be another one along momentarily to show him the way.

This was very rough and hilly terrain, he told himself, marveling a little until he remembered that it must be the spaded flower bed under the kitchen windows. Earlier that spring, Craig himself had helped with the spading of this particular bed, and he hadn't been too careful about breaking up clods. He wished now that he had been. There wouldn't be so many steep hills to climb.

Then he discovered that he had gone as far as was necessary. At this point, a sufficient distance from their doorway, the ants were depositing their loads, dropping the fragments where they mingled and blended unnoticed in the spaded soil. Craig dropped his burden, too, with a sigh of relief, and sat down on an overlooked boulder, which he reminded himself was probably really only a small pebble, to rest.

With twitching antennae, which expressed their disapproval more eloquently than words, the engineers passed him by as, empty jawed, they hurried back to their underground project. Craig knew that there was scorn behind their milky white eyes, disdain in every glistening line of their black bodies, but he didn't care. He was tired. He had to catch his breath and rest a minute before he could go on.

He leaned his head wearily against the thick green trunk of a tree which grew nearby. It was a tall tree, and the foliage started high up above his head, so far up that it appeared as only green and scarlet splotches against the deep blue sky.

Then, without warning, the sky was covered with something huge and dark and flat, like a heavy, threatening board. It descended closer and closer until everything else was blotted out. Craig could no longer see the sky, nor the tree trunk, only that gigantic board coming nearer, ready to crush him. Just in the nick of time he rolled off the pebble, and crawled and scratched his way to safety as the board pressed flat against the ground where he had been sitting.

"Grace, your zinnias are lovely this year," exclaimed a great booming voice. "Just look at this red one!"

As Craig stared up, another vast board descended to the ground, settling close to the first one, only now he realized what they were. They weren't boards at all, but the leather soles of shoes. Peoples' shoes. Shoes belonging to human beings who were still their normal sizes, not reduced as was he to the stature of an ant.

Two more shoes, huge and formidable and frightening, swooped down to rest beside the others, and this time Craig recognized his mother's voice.

"They have done well. Let me pick you a bouquet, Ruth."

"Mother! Mother!" he shrieked as loudly as he could. "Mother, it's me! Craig!"

If she heard, she did not answer. The tall tree trunk beside him bent and cracked as she broke off its flowery top.

"Mother! It's Craig. Your boy," he tried again, screaming as loudly as he could. Apparently his voice, like his body, had grown so small that it was no longer audible to the human ear.

Since he could not make her hear, he realized that he must do something else to attract her attention, and, moving cautiously, fearful that any moment she might change her footing and crush him, he managed to leap from the ground to the side of her slipper. For a moment he clung there, afraid he would slide back, then he managed to crawl up until he was sitting on her instep. From there he crept up to her ankle, where he paused and gave a series of quick pats.

Immediately she lifted her foot and shook it so violently that it was all he could do to cling on.

"Goodness," he heard her say. "The bugs are terrible this year. It's hardly safe to come outside. Jim's going to have to spray again."

Then she bent down, and with her hand brushed him roughly to the ground. He lay there gasping for the breath which had been knocked from his body with the fall, and Aunt Ruth's voice came to him again.

"That's plenty, Grace. Really it is."

"Well, if you're sure," said Mother. "But you know you're welcome to all you want."

Again he saw the huge black boards blotting out parts of the blue sky as the two women turned and left the flower bed. They came perilously close to him, but neither quite closed down.

The next moment, antennae prodded his forehead irritably.

"Come along, lazy creature," ordered Digger. "There's work to be done, and there are Mashers about. Hurry, or they'll grind you underfoot."

"I'm coming," agreed Craig sadly. He got up, and trotted after the ant as rapidly as his aching body would permit.

5

WHEN JILL FOLLOWED NANNIE into the nursery, she was thinking of Craig rather than the babies she was expected to tend.

"I hope he doesn't get into any trouble," she said aloud. "He says things he doesn't mean, sometimes, and goodness knows what will happen to him without me along."

Nannie's sharp side eye had observed the movement of Jill's lips and immediately she stopped and placed her antennae on the girl's head.

"I imagine you are commenting upon the scientific procedure of our nursery. My Lady told me that you love babies and are anxious to work with them instead of living the slothful life of a pet. We are glad to welcome you, and I'm sure we can find enough hard work to keep you very happy."

"Thank you, Nannie," said Jill quickly. "I've never done much baby sitting before. People always seemed to think I was too young. But I'd like to learn."

"You shall. You shall," approved Nannie. "How old are you?"

"Ten."

"Ten years?" Nannie's antennae vibrated with shock. "Your age is not the reason why you have never tended babies. You are a queen."

"No. I'm just a little girl."

"You must be a queen," insisted Nannie firmly. "Only queens live so long. Workers seldom live beyond seven years. I, myself, am six, and I've been tending babies ever since I was one myself. I've a great talent for it, you see, so I've stayed on in the nursery training others."

"You must be very capable to be in charge of all the nurses," Jill told her respectfully.

"Oh, I am but one of several who share the responsibility. Still, it is a great honor," confessed Nannie. "Our babies are the most important thing in the City, you know. They must be cared for, and protected, at any cost, even to our lives."

"Of course," said Jill politely.

She turned and looked around the room, wondering exactly where the babies were kept, for at first glance, not one was in sight. Against one wall was a stack of tiny white eggs, similar to those which the nursemaids had carried from the queen's apartment. They were piled in neat rows, and graduated in size, the smaller ones at one end, the larger eggs at the opposite. Before them, a group of ants moved up and down the line, licking each egg with flicking black tongues.

"Babies have to eat," explained Nannie tolerantly, following her gaze. "They're always hungry."

"That's what I've always heard," agreed Jill uncertainly. "And they have to be kept clean, too. I guess that's what those nurses are doing over there, isn't it? Washing the eggs?"

"Dear me, no," Nannie's antennae twitched with amusement at the idea. "The eggs are already clean. As I just told you, they're being fed. Come along and I'll show you."

One or two of the nurses gave Jill a side glance when they reached the rows of eggs, but most of them continued their work without seeming to notice that they were being observed.

"These are the newest babies," explained Nannie, pointing with one front foot toward the smallest eggs. "They were just laid today. Aren't they cunning? And there, at the opposite end, are the older babies who have had many days of feeding. They've grown quite fat and healthy on their formulae, as you can see. They're nearly ready to hatch into dear little larvae."

"What is their formulae, Nannie?" asked Jill. She didn't like to admit that she had never heard of eggs growing larger once they had been laid, but then she didn't see how they could be fed, either. There were certainly no bottles or feeding equipment of any kind.

"Milk, naturally." Nannie gave her a quick look from her three pearly eyes, then added kindly, "I see now why you were never trusted with babies. You really don't know the first thing about them, do you?" She paused, her antennae vibrating sensitively, then she turned to the nursemaids. "This room will soon be too chilly for the eggs. They must be moved to Nursery 7 immediately!"

At once each nurse grasped an egg in her mouth and scurried out the door with it.

"You have more than one nursery?" asked Jill curiously.

"Oh, many of them. We move things around constantly. It's a matter of temperature, you know. And then it gives us a sense of security, too. If we should be attacked, the enemy would have to hunt for the nursery. Sometimes even I have trouble remembering just where it is at the moment. Now, come along and see the little larvae. They're being fed, too."

The larvae, so many that she couldn't even begin to count them, were also being licked by their nurses, and Jill rightly concluded that the formulae, whatever it was, was contained in the nannies' mouths. Although she was careful not to say so, she didn't consider this stage of ant babies very pretty. The larvae were gourd-shaped, and looked like little white, hairy worms, soft and squashy and without eyes. They had mouths, though, and from some of these openings protruded gossamer threads, like the webs a spider might spin. As Jill watched, the strands grew longer and longer. Nannie was excited when she saw them.

"Will you look at that!" she marveled. "Such precocious babies! Already they're changing into pupae!"

With a shuddering movement, one of the white wormlike creatures exhaled a long strand of pale silk, then rolled over and over until it was completely wrapped in the thread.

"Oh, careful!" cried Jill in alarm. "It may choke itself, Nannie."

"Bless your heart, no," denied Nannie kindly. "That's what it's supposed to do. Soon it will spin enough silk so that it's wrapped up as neatly as a little sack, and then it will be a pupa. They're over here, if you'd care to see them."

It was not necessary to feed the pupae. In fact, it would have been impossible to do so, for they were nothing but little cocoons of tightly wrapped thread. Laid out in neat rows, they looked like so many white packages, and there was no visible evidence of the pale sightless worm inside.

"There'll be just time for you to go to the Delivery Room and see the new babies coming out of their pupae before we go to the pasture for a new supply of milk," confided Nannie. "We get our milk straight from the cows, to make sure that it's fresh. That's why I didn't put you to work at once. I wasn't sure that the milk in your crop was fresh enough for babies."

"My crop?" repeated Jill foolishly. "Where is my crop?"

"Inside you, silly. It's your second stomach, a little bag that holds the extra food you don't need yourself, the food that you

57

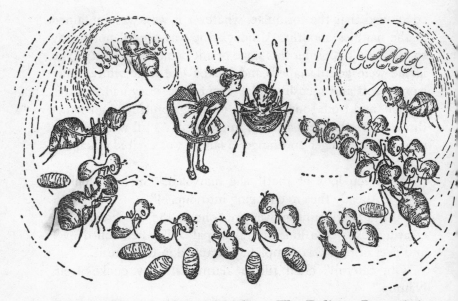

share with others. Now come along. The Delivery Room is in another chamber."

Nannie turned and hurried away, and Jill trotted after her as fast as she could. The suggestion that she was expected to have a crop, a little bag to hold milk for the ant babies, was really upsetting. So far, Nannie had been very kind, but that was because she expected Jill to do her part as a nursemaid later on. She might not be so happy when she discovered that Jill had no little bag in which to carry a supply of milk.

The Delivery Room was a busy place, and not nearly so neat and well organized as the other parts of the nursery. Here there was almost a state of confusion. The cocoons were no longer piled in orderly rows, but were scattered here and there about the floor, and the nurses darted this way and that, trying to see to everything at once. Most of the cocoons were moving, and while some only gave an occasional twitch or jerk, others were tossing and heaving like bits of exploding corn in a popper. Here and there lay an empty pupa, a flat tangle of matted threads on the brown floor, and beside it rested its recent occupant, a white worm no longer, but a tiny dark insect, similar to the larger ants, but with a strange soft look to its body.

"Oh, there are the babies," cried Jill in excitement. "But they shouldn't be left there on the floor, poor things. They might get cold."

"Don't touch them!" Nannie pulled her back with a jerk of her capable front leg. "They haven't been out long enough for their skins to harden. Give them a little while, then it will be perfectly safe to fondle them." But it seemed that her milky eyes were filled with pleased understanding. "Now here's one that's ready to come out, and needs help."

Jill followed her to one of the vigorously heaving cocoons, and stood staring as Nannie crouched over it, holding it still with one of her feet. She opened her mouth and gently, carefully, her sharp teeth tore at the silk threads until there was a tiny hole. A moment later, the opening was filled with a dark head which moved this way and that, ripping the silk strands until there was room for the whole body to slip through.

"Cunning, isn't it?" asked Nannie proudly. "We have to help them, poor dears. They have such a time getting started."

"Are they fed pretty soon?" asked Jill, staring at the newly emerged baby.

"Not here. They'll be strong enough to walk soon, then they'll be taken to another nursery to be washed and fed. They mustn't be touched until then."

Jill smiled smugly to herself. This was the proper place for her to work, a place where she wouldn't be expected to supply formulae for hungry babies.

"Do you suppose I could work here?" she asked Nannie. "These nurses have almost more than they can do."

"Indeed you can," approved Nannie promptly. "Of course we're not always having such a rush as this, and there may be a few idle moments when you're bored. But I'm glad that you're anxious to keep busy."

"Shall I start now?"

Nannie's antennae twitched thoughtfully.

"No," she decided after a moment. "It's time for my group to milk the cows. You'd better come with me to the pasture and see how that's done. It's better for you to learn everything at once, then I won't have to stop and answer your questions later."

"All right," agreed Jill reluctantly. "But I hope they won't all be hatched by the time I get back, and they won't need me."

"Don't worry about that," Nannie assured her. "There are new babies every day. The City must go on, you know."

There were a dozen nurses who set off on the expedition to the pasture, and Nannie explained that it was usual to send out only small groups at a time. That way the eggs and larvae and pupae were never left completely untended. They left the nursery together, but almost immediately Jill fell far behind, for she couldn't possibly keep up with the others. There was nothing to do but continue on as fast as she could, but it was a little frightening to be all alone in the tunnel. In a few moments, however, Nannie came racing back.

"Can't you run any faster than this, my dear?" she demanded with concern.

"I'm afraid not," Jill admitted sadly.

"Then there's nothing to do but carry you," decided Nannie, and as though in answer to her unspoken command, four other nurses returned and silently lifted Jill as the soldiers had done. Nannie led the way, and they all proceeded down the tunnel at great speed.

At the entrance way to the Great Hall, Jill had a glimpse of a crowd of ants who seemed to be making the opening wider, but there was no time for more than a quick glance before she was whisked by. She waved to Cricket across the room, and Cricket waved back, immediately afterwards unfurling his wings and giving out with an enthusiastic "Crick, crick, crick," which bounced back and forth in echoes against the earth walls.

At the ramp, Nannie brushed the sentinels aside with her antennae, and they respectfully fell back to let the party pass. They were not the only ones journeying to the outer world, Jill observed, for their group joined and blended with a solid line of laborers who were transporting something in their jaws, but the passageway grew dark almost immediately so she could not see what they were carrying outside.

Jill had been amazed when Nannie told her that the ants obtained milk directly from cows, but there had been no chance to question her about it further. Now, as they climbed the dark hill, she thought of it again, and wondered how far they would have to go for milk once they were outside. Craig's home was in a residential district, and so far as Jill knew, cows weren't kept in the city limits. Perhaps she had been foolish to leave the nursery for so long; Craig might come looking for her. Even though the ants ran at top speed, a journey to the country would take several days. The thought was so disturbing that she reached over in the darkness, groping until her fingers found the spiraling rod of an antenna.

"Are the cows very far from here? Will it take us a long time?"

"Not far," came the answer. "The herd used by the nursery is pastured quite near the entrance."

"The herd? You mean there's more than one cow?" Jill's surprised voice boomed against the walls of the tunnel.

"Certainly. There are more than one of us, aren't there?" The antenna throbbed impatiently. "I would appreciate it if you wouldn't distract me right now with communications. I need my antennae to show me the way I should be going."

"Excuse me," said Jill quickly.

Once they were out of the tunnel and into the sunlight, she expected to be put down. Instead, at a signal from Nannie, the four who were carrying her set off over the stone highway. They skirted the edge of the exotic green forest, close enough so that tall fronds waving above their heads cast refreshing shadows in the path. Suddenly, without warning, the ant who was carrying Jill's left leg, dropped it. The other three had been unprepared, and for a moment she hung there, her leg and hip scraping the rough stone. Then they had pulled her after them into the cool green dusk of the forest.

"What is it? What happened?" she demanded.

The antennae of the nurse beside her moved ever so slightly. "Sh," she warned. "Be still. An enemy."

Cautiously, Jill moved one of the green blades. Through the opening she could see part of the highway, and there, standing perfectly still in the opening, was the most terrifying figure she had ever seen. It was like a caricature in a parade, one of those giant, inflated figures on stilts that bounce along above the heads of the crowd, and are neither quite man nor beast. It had a huge, armless body, covered with gigantic black and gray feathers, even the smallest of which was larger than ostrich plumes, only unlike fluffy ostrich feathers, these were straight and spiny. The great feathered head was tilted to one side, as though the creature might be listening, and the sunlight picked up a glitter from a wicked black eye which was as big as Jill herself. The creature's face ended in a sharp, yellow snout, which seemed to be composed of hard bone or shell, and as she stared in horrified fascination the two sides swung open, and she could see that it was really a beak, a beak so large that it could easily swallow their whole party at a single gulp. Almost as terrifying as its beak were the legs, scaly and yellow, with clawlike rays shooting out at the bottom. She shivered, knowing instinctively that if one of those tremendous feet came down upon her it would crush the breath from her body, and break every bone as well.

Then the beak opened once more, and this time the great throat swelled as the creature spoke twice, before unfurling gigantic wings to fly away.

"Chirp, chirp!"

"My goodness," exclaimed Jill in shocked amazement. "It was a bird. A sparrow, maybe."

Nannie began checking off the members of her party by touching one after another with her antennae.

"One casualty," she announced. "Come, it is safe now to go on to the pasture."

The nurse who had been carrying Jill's left leg was missing, and she couldn't help shivering when she realized what a close call it had been. Had the nurse clung tight to her burden, Jill, too, might have been gobbled up by the sparrow.

Nannie took the place of the missing nursemaid, and the little party continued on its way. After a while they left the highway and struck off through a little path between the green fronds. It was delightfully cool in here, and the filtered sunlight made everything look as though they were traveling under water. Once they encountered a large angular insect which, upon spying them, immediately leaped away on tremendously long legs like tree trunks, and Jill realized it was a grasshopper. Another time they passed a motionless gray slug, whereupon Nannie's antennae wrinkled hungrily and she demanded crossly what was the foraging party thinking of to let good meat lie around that way?

Jill was just beginning to think that the ant had been mistaken in saying that the cows were close to the City, when they stopped. As she was set carefully on the ground, she saw that they had come out of the lush jungle into a round clearing of sandy soil. In the very center grew a mighty tree, the trunk of which was thicker than her own body.

"Can you climb?" asked Nannie, touching her delicately, and pointing to the tree.

"I hope so," Jill told her, looking doubtfully at the green trunk. "I'm more used to trees that have branches closer to the ground, but I'll try."

"I'll climb behind you and boost," promised Nannie. "Just follow the others."

The other nurses had already begun running up the tree trunk, their six little feet clinging to the wood in a way which Jill could not help but envy. She started climbing herself, and was delighted that it was not so difficult as she had imagined. There were occasional bumps to which she could hold, the rubber soles of her tennis shoes were a help, and whenever she got stuck, there was Nannie to push her on over the slippery place. Eventually they reached the crotch of the tree, where three limbs spiralled out in as many directions.

"Ah," said Nannie, tickling Jill gently. "This is one of our best pastures. And how do you like the herd? Isn't it a fine one? We raised these ourselves, kept them in the underground stable and fed them ensilage through the winter. They're our prize stock."

Jill's eyes opened in amazement as they followed along the branches to the outer limbs. The leaves of each limb were thick with fat green insects, which seemed to be gorging themselves on the juices. Each ant, upon arrival, had selected one of the creatures, and was now stroking it gently on the abdomen. As Jill watched, a tiny glistening drop appeared on the green skin, whereupon the ant licked it up and moved on to another green insect where the process was repeated.

"What are they?" she gasped.

"Cows," Nannie told her impatiently. "Surely you've seen cows before. Sometimes they're known as aphids, but cow is a much better name. Come, here's a fat one. She'll have lots of milk, and I'm sure you're thirsty."

Nannie expertly stroked the fat aphid a time or two, and when a white drop appeared on one of the tiny tubercles on its abdomen, she motioned to Jill to drink.

For a moment Jill hesitated. She loved milk, but it had always been served to her in a glass. Then she saw Nannie's eyes upon her, and she bent her head. To her amazement, the liquid proved to be delicious. It had the texture of real milk, but with a sweet honeylike taste.

"There," approved Nannie. "You know how to do it, so you can milk your own cows after this. Drink lots. Fill your crop. Remember the babies."

It was rather fun milking the little green aphids. Like cows they were gentle, and seemed almost grateful for the attention. They stood quite still while the milking was going on, but when it was finished they fell to feeding again as placidly as before. Among them wandered their herders, the cowgirls, important little ants who had brought the aphids here to pasture, and stayed to look after them.

"I wonder what kind of tree this is that they use for pasture," mused Jill, and wandered farther out on the limb where a great splotch of crimson coloring had caught her eye. As she drew nearer, her nose was filled with a familiar fragrance. Roses! Why, this was Aunt Grace's favorite rosebush. Just ahead was one of the blossoms, huge and cool and velvety smooth.

She crept closer, smelling the delicious sweetness which the sunshine drew forth. She had smelled it before, only it was never like this, never so strong and penetrating. Then she felt a strong leg clamp itself around her arm, and the next moment she was pulled inside the blossom.

"Be quiet," whispered Nannie. "Don't wiggle. There's a wasp about, but he'll never find us here."

Jill slid down between two smooth scented petals beside Nannie. She sensed that whatever was about to happen was dangerous, and she took tiny breaths lest she flutter one of the delicate petals. She could hear the wasp now. It made a noise like a jet plane, and it must be swooping and buzzing quite near at hand.

"What is he doing?" she whispered.

"Eating some of our sisters," said Nannie sadly. "Those who have forgotten the law."

"The law?"

"Eat without being eaten, and protect the babies. That wasp

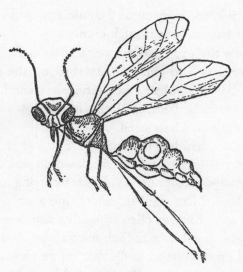

knew we had cows pastured here. He's probably been waiting until there were enough of us to make his raid worth while. Don't communicate. Just be quiet until he goes away."

It seemed to Jill that the noise of the wasp outside the rose would never stop. Sometimes it was very close, and at other times it drifted farther away, then it grew loud again. Nannie lay perfectly still on the red petal, and Jill realized that it was the first time she had ever seen an ant remain entirely motionless. She, too, lay as quietly as possible, but her mind was not quiet. She wondered what terrible things were going on outside. Obviously the wasp was an enemy of the ants. How many of their little party had he devoured by this time? And what of the cows? Had he gobbled them, too?

After what seemed a very long time indeed, the buzzing outside grew softer, and eventually it faded away entirely. Nannie stirred herself vigorously, as though to make up for lost time.

"He's gone. Let's hope that all of our party were law-abiding citizens and kept out of his way. Come along now."

She crawled out of the rose, and Jill followed, her mind completely bewildered. How could Nannie remain so calm while she and her friends were in such peril?

Apparently the wasp had not been interested in the aphids, for they continued to graze undisturbed on the green stems and leaves. Ants, who had taken refuge in some hiding place, were now crawling back, and the milking was resumed as though nothing had happened.

Jill, however, had lost her appetite. She was still trembling from her recent fright, and she sat down on one of the green leaves to rest and recover herself. It was terrifying to be so small that birds looked like giant monsters, and a wasp represented more than an itching, swollen sting. She wondered if she and Craig would ever get back to their normal size, or if they would be gobbled up or crushed underfoot before such a thing happened. She didn't see how the ants could stand it. How could they exist day and night in constant fear of their lives?

The wind ruffled the leaf next to her, giving her a view of a dozen fat green cows contentedly munching on the underside. Beside them a busy nursemaid had just finished lapping up a white droplet. Impulsively, Jill leaned over and touched the black antennae with a gentle finger.

"How can you eat so soon after your scare?" she asked curiously. "I should think your stomach would be too upset. Mine is."

"Why should my stomach be upset?" asked the ant in surprise.

"Because of the wasp. Didn't he frighten you? Weren't you scared?"

"I don't know what you mean," confessed the nurse. "I have never heard those words before."

"What words?"

"Frighten. Scare. What do they mean?"

"They're what you feel when you see danger coming," said

68

Jill a little uncertainly. "What did you think about when you heard the wasp coming?"

"I remembered the law, of course," the ant told her promptly. "Eat without being eaten." As though that concluded the discussion, she ran down the stem and out onto another leaf.

Jill got up, too. She decided that the best thing for her to do was to find Nannie, and stay close to her. The other nurses, while not unfriendly, would not put themselves out on Jill's account. They might not even warn her of danger should another enemy present itself. She walked out onto the limb, being careful not to look down lest the great height make her dizzy.

As she stood there, wondering which way to go, she heard another sound. It was not the jet-plane noise of the wasp, but a rasping little buzz, and a moment later a round orange object with black wings settled down beside her. For a moment Jill was afraid she would lose her footing, and she wavered uncertainly on the branch, but the rubber soles of her shoes clung tightly, and when the limb stopped swaying, she saw that it was only an orange beetle which had alighted beside her.

"Ladybug!" she exclaimed in a pleased voice, grateful that here was no enemy. Lady beetles were harmless. She had picked up hundreds of them in the days when she was her normal size, and chanted the old rhyme about flying away home because their houses were on fire.

True, it looked more dangerous now that she was seeing it in this perspective, but it still wasn't too alarming. It resembled an orange enameled armored truck, and ignoring her completely, it began crawling toward one of the leaves which was heavy with green aphids.

"Save the cows! Save the cows!" cried one of the cowgirls, brushing against Jill, and pausing long enough to give the order. "There's a beetle in the pasture! Help save the cows!"

Jill stood staring stupidly. All around her were signs of great agitation. The herders were driving droves of green aphids before them, in from the leaves and down the stalks. The nurses had left off milking, and seemed to be leaving, too. She turned once more to glance toward the orange ladybug, who had just arrived at her destination. As Jill stared in growing horror, the ponderous jaw gaped open and closed shut. Three of the tiny green aphids disappeared from the leaf as it happened.

"Why, you mean ladybug," cried Jill indignantly. "Those little aphids never hurt you. It's one thing to drink milk, but it's not fair to gobble the cows that give it!"

She dashed out onto the next leaf where another herd of aphids grazed contentedly, unaware of the threatening danger.

"Shoo! Shoo!" Jill cried, trying to push them from their pasture and out onto the stem as she had seen the herders do. But there was a knack to herding ant-cows which she did not know. The little aphids clung tightly, and refused to budge. She glanced across to the opposite leaf. It was empty of aphids by this time, and the orange armored car was turning to move on. She bent down and picked up the aphids, one after another. The herd on this leaf just filled her two pockets to the brim. Then she hurried back to the crotch of the rosebush, and there was Nannie, waiting for her.

"Come, come," ordered Nannie, her antennae waggling furiously. "We must return to the City."

"But the ladybug—she'll kill all the cows!"

"The herders will have to look after them," said Nannie firmly. "I only hope they can save enough of this prize stock for a new start. But that is their problem, not ours. We must return to the nursery with the fresh milk for the babies."

She whisked Jill down the trunk so rapidly that there was no time to mention the green cows in her pockets. Nor could she speak of them when they reached the ground, for here were four ants, waiting to snatch her up before setting off through the green jungle.

Nannie had preceded them, and was waiting at the entrance

to the City when they arrived. She touched each nursemaid lightly with the tips of her antennae.

"You're the last," she announced. "Twelve of us set out. Eight returned. That makes four who allowed themselves to be eaten."

"But I'm sure they couldn't help it," gasped Jill.

"That's no excuse," said Nannie firmly. "No excuse at all. They broke the law."

6

CRAIG PAUSED AT THE ENTRANCE to the tunnel leading down to the ant city, and took a deep breath. He didn't see how he could make himself return for another heavy load of earth. His legs were tired, his arms ached, and when no one was looking he had cried a little after the disappointment of not being recognized by his own mother.

As he stood there, trying to get up courage to step out of the sun into the darkness of the tunnel, an important little ant bustled around the corner of the steps. Her antennae waved wildly, and her black legs fairly flew over the ground as she darted from one to another of the engineers who were making for the opening.

"Food! Food! A fine catch to be hauled in! Come along. I'll need help here."

Along with the others, she had prodded Craig as she scurried by, perhaps not even noticing, in her excitement, that he was different from the rest. Then she turned and hurried back the way she had come, across the gray highway and into the waving green forest beyond. And after her raced each ant she had summoned.

Craig reached out and detained the last worker as she was about to leave.

"Does she mean me, too?" he demanded. "Aren't we supposed to go after more dirt?"

"That was Grubber, one of the foragers," the engineer told him impatiently. "When one of the grubbers calls for help in bringing in food, everything else must wait. It's part of the law."

She jerked loose, and before Craig could question her further, had scurried off after the others, her waving antennae smelling out the way.

Craig made an instant choice and followed. He had no experience with bringing food into the City, but he had tried hauling dirt out of it, and he didn't enjoy it.

The engineer had disappeared between the waving green fronds on the other side of the pavement long before Craig had crossed over, but he tried to make a mental note of the spot, and was pleased to see, when he arrived, that there was a little trail. It was not much wider than his own body, and once he was upon it he had the feeling of being completely shut in. The green stalks (it was hard to remember they were only grasses, when they towered above his head) grew so thickly on either side that he could not see to right or left. When the wind blew, he had occasional glimpses of blue sky, but mostly the stems closed overhead in a lacing archway, and because the trail turned and bent, he was unable to see very far ahead, nor could he see where he had been. There was only one thing to do on a trail like this: just keep on, and hope that he didn't run into a place where it forked.

Even as he thought about such a danger, it was upon him. He arrived at a spot where the green stems parted in two directions. One trail went straight ahead, while a second veered off to the left. If he had been an ant, he told himself ruefully, he would have no trouble at all. He could wave his antennae a few times and pick up the vanillalike scent of his companions. But without that faculty, it would be very easy to get lost in this waving green jungle. He might never be found at all, but just go wandering around until someone came to cut the grass. And when that happened, he would certainly be crushed under the roller of the lawnmower.

So long as he remained his present size, his only safety lay in remaining with the ants. Well, they would have to return this way, no matter which fork they had taken, and the best thing to do was wait for them here. He sat down on the ground so that he could keep an eye on both trails. He hoped they would hurry, for he suddenly realized he was very hungry.

He was thinking so hard that he didn't hear anyone come up behind him, and it was not until he felt the ends of antennae tickling his neck that he realized he was no longer alone.

"Who are you? You have the smell of our City upon you, but you are not one of our sisters," said a voice in his ear.

Craig jumped up and whirled around. Blocking the trail down which he had come was an ant. At first glance he might not have observed that she was different in any way from the other inhabitants of the City, but when he looked again he realized that this one was very different indeed.

Her hard black coat lacked polish, as though she had been too careless to wash herself properly, or that she didn't consider it important. Her waist was as slim and graceful as My Lady's, but it was a muscular slimness, as though it was kept trimmed down by hard exercise. She was not fat, like Nannie, nor were her jaws and forelegs so ponderous as those of Digger or the soldiers, but they moved more quickly, as though she could be depended upon to get herself out of the way of her enemies. Like the other ants, it was impossible to read any expression on

74

her features, and yet somehow she gave the impression of being self-sufficient, fearless, and perhaps even a little calculating.

"My name's Craig," he told her. "I'm a b— I mean, I'm a—a Masher. Your queen made my cousin and me small like this."

"What for?" demanded the ant instantly. "What use did she have for you?"

"I'm not sure," admitted Craig honestly. "I think she was just mad at us, only she's too busy right now to change us back. At first we were supposed to be pets. You know, like Cricket. But we didn't want to be that, so my cousin's helping in the nursery, and I've been working with the engineers."

"What are you doing out here?"

"Somebody named Grubber came along and told us to come help carry some food. But the others got ahead of me, and I didn't know which way they'd gone, so I decided to wait here."

The wiry ant flicked her antennae a few times in the air, then pointed them to the left fork.

"They went that way."

"Thank you," said Craig politely standing up. Now that he knew the way, he should follow after the others, but for some reason he was reluctant to leave this new acquaintance. She was the first ant he had met with whom he seemed able to get along.

"Do you mind telling me your name?" he asked diffidently.

"I'm Nosy. I'm a scout."

"That must be very interesting work," Craig admired. "I wish I could be a scout."

"I don't see how you could," said Nosy frankly. "Apparently you've no sense of smell at all, or you wouldn't have lost your way."

"I can smell some things," insisted Craig.

"Like sugar?" demanded Nosy.

"Well, some kinds of sugar," admitted Craig, trying to think if there were any odor at all to a sugar bowl. "I can smell chocolate candy, and honey, and things like that. And of course I can smell sour things, like vinegar and dill pickles——"

"What's the use of smelling those? They aren't good to eat," argued Nosy. "Can you smell danger?"

"I don't think I ever did."

"To be a scout, you must smell danger. Poisons are danger. Sometimes they're disguised by sugar, and it's hard for any but the best scout to scent them out."

"I'll bet they never fool you, though," Craig told her, remembering that Jill had advised him to use flattery. "No matter how much sugar they put in it."

"Well, I'm still here," pointed out Nosy. "I've a particularly keen nose for the cinnamon scent of the red ants."

"You mean red ants smell like cinnamon?"

"Not all red ants, naturally. Some smell like cooked cabbage, and others like sage dressing. But our particular enemy, the red ants who live under the hydrangea bush, smell like cinnamon. It's a disgusting odor."

"Do you mind if we don't talk about food," asked Craig. "When I think of it, it makes my stomach hurt, I'm so hungry."

"Why didn't you say so?" demanded Nosy promptly. She took two steps forward until she stood directly in front of him. "Open your mouth."

Obediently Craig opened his mouth, and a moment later it was filled with sweet liquid. He swallowed, and it felt warm and comforting going down.

"What was that?"

"Oh, let me think," said Nosy thoughtfully. "It's been in my crop since lunch, and I've almost forgotten what I ate. It was probably grub. That's what I generally have when I'm scouting in the field."

"A grub?" Craig gulped. But no matter what he thought

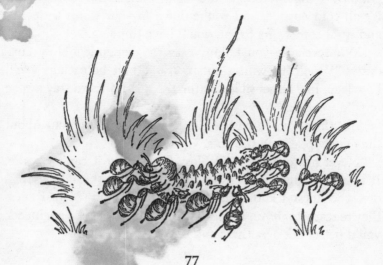

about eating grubs, it had tasted good at the time, and his stomach was feeling pleasantly full once more.

"Let's run along and see how they're getting along with the food," suggested Nosy, turning down the trail. She took it for granted that Craig could follow, and because he didn't want to be left alone again he hurried after her as fast as he could.

They came upon the foraging party just around the second bend. The catch filled the whole trail, and the engineers had been busy digging out a little space at each side to give them a better footing. It was a large, soft, gray slug, and it seemed to be swimming in a pale watery fluid.

"What's that?" demanded Craig, tugging at Nosy and pointing to the liquid.

"Ant acid," replied Nosy. "We wouldn't want such good food to get away, would we? The acid will keep it quiet until we're ready to move it to the City."

"Is it poison?"

"Not to us," Nosy's antennae twitched jauntily. "Of course it didn't help the slug."

"It'll be fine food for next winter, won't it?" asked Craig politely, trying not to look at the gray mass in the trail. "When it's all cold outside, and you're down in your warm little city and want something to eat, you'll have this slug."

"Whatever are you talking about?" demanded Nosy curiously. "When it's winter outside, we won't be eating. We'll be asleep, like all sensible creatures. Who wants to stay awake in cold weather?"

"But the story," persisted Craig. "You know, the one about the grasshopper and the ants?"

"Never heard of it," said Nosy firmly. "So it can't be true. It's probably just one of those rumors that get started by someone who doesn't know what he's talking about. Well, I guess they're ready to move. If you're supposed to help the engineers, you'd better get over there and carry your share."

78

For once Craig considered that he had things easier than the ants. The slug was too heavy to lift off the ground, and they had to push and pull it along. It was much simpler for him to manage his share of the load, using his two hands, than it was for the ants, who grasped it in their jaws. Moreover, the weight slowed down their usual speed, so that it was not difficult for him to keep up with the others.

Nosy helped pull whenever the slug stuck on a grass root, but generally she walked along in front as befitted the dignity of a scout. From time to time, the ants, by unspoken consent, paused to rest, and whenever this happened, Nosy returned to Craig. She seemed to have a feeling of curiosity about him which was not shared by the others.

"Do you like to be a Masher?" she inquired.

"Yes."

"Why? What can Mashers do that we can't?"

"Oh, lots of things," Craig assured her quickly. "We play, and look at television, and read books, and go to the movies, and ride bikes, and——"

"I don't know what any of those are," admitted Nosy. "Do Mashers have to have them? Can't they get along without them?"

"I suppose so. But they're nice to have."

"Let's stick to the important things," she insisted. "Do you always have food?"

"Of course."

"Do you have grubbers to go out and find it for you? And herds of cows that you go out to milk?"

"We get our food at stores," Craig told her. "Even the milk. We don't have to look for it. It's just there, and we go get what we want."

"Don't they try to stop you? Put out poison?"

"Oh, we pay for it," he explained quickly. "We give the store money before we take anything."

"And where do you get this thing called money?" Her three eyes stared into his face intently.

"You have to work for it."

"Work, of course," Nosy agreed, her antennae twitching with understanding. "Food, shelter, and work. The same things are important to us."

The pauses for rest grew more frequent, and it became clear that the ants would never be able to haul the heavy slug over this narrow trail. The thick growth at each side caught, and it took too much strength to break it down. The grubbers and Nosy held a consultation, at the conclusion of which the scout pushed her way through a thicket and disappeared. The others waited patiently where they were, only moving when the slug gave an indication that it might break loose.

After some time, Nosy returned, pushing her way through the green blades with a sinuous dexterity.

"I've found a much wider trail," she announced triumphantly. "It will be hard going for only a little way. You'll have to dig yourself a road to the intersection, but once we reach there, you'll have no more trouble."

Immediately the grubbers became engineers again. Nosy showed them the way, and they began building a little road between the grass. It was not a straight road, for it had to wind around the thickest clumps, but it was amazing to Craig how quickly it began to take form. With their heavy jaws they hollowed out a trench, and because the surplus did not have to be carried far away, but could be dumped to one side, the results were soon visible.

Craig was expected to help. He was glad now that his mother had insisted that the lawn be watered every evening, for the ground was not too hard. He could scratch it loose with his fingernails, and really didn't need the knife in his pocket. But when he found himself confronted by a sturdy clump of grass, he took it out and cut each blade level with the soil. Nosy came up behind him just as he was finishing.

"What are you doing?" she demanded. "Are you hungry again? Did you think there were seeds in the top of those grasses that might be good to eat?"

"No," Craig told her. "I'm just getting it out of the way so we won't have to waste time going around it."

"Very ingenious," admitted Nosy. "No doubt it's something you learned as a Masher."

She raced off to call the attention of the others to what Craig had done, but none of them seemed to share her enthusiasm. No engineer bothered to compliment him, nor was he asked to clear any more grass out of their way. They continued their excavating as they had always done, and the road curved and bent as it grew.

After a time they came out on the second trail which was, as Nosy had promised, much wider than the first. As a matter of fact it was nearly as wide as the pavement by the back steps, and Craig recognized it immediately. It was a trail, worn by his own feet and those of his friends, which led up to the apple tree swing. With much tugging and pushing, the gray slug was hoisted out of the grass and onto the sandy trail, and the little band of ants once more took up their positions to move it downhill toward the City.

"Tell me," said Nosy, coming to stand beside Craig and regarding him earnestly. "What do Mashers think of their babies? Do they protect them?"

"Oh, yes indeed. Our babies are very well cared for," Craig assured her.

"Good," said Nosy, and stepped out of the way to give Craig room to lift his share of the slug. A moment later, she began to teeter, as though the sand beneath her feet was giving way. Then she disappeared completely from view.

Craig took his hands from the slug and stared after her. He

couldn't imagine where she had gone, unless she had fallen into a hole in the sand. If that was the case, surely it was the duty of the engineers to help her out. She could be badly hurt.

The ant on his right leaned over and jabbed him impatiently.

"Hurry, hurry," she ordered. "Pick up your load. Didn't you see what happened? We must get out of here before the ant lion gets us all."

"Ant lion?"

"The one in the hole. The one that just got Nosy." The antennae rapped impatiently against his cheek. "This road isn't safe. Hurry."

"I'm not going to leave Nosy," cried Craig angrily. "I'm going to help her. And you ought to, too."

Without answering, the ant moved ahead. The grubbing party was proceeding on to the City with the supply of meat.

Craig hurried to the spot where he had seen Nosy disappear. He was expecting a hole, since the scout must have fallen into one, but he was upon it before he realized. The sand, which looked so solid just ahead, began crumbling under his feet, and he couldn't keep himself from falling. Once the uppercrust gave way, he was on a steep slope which made him tumble and roll a few times before he reached the bottom. But even when he was no longer falling, he continued to move from side to side, and his back, under his tee-shirt began to itch and sting.

At first he thought he must have landed on a stickery plant which was being blown about, but a moment later he realized that he had fallen directly onto the broad back of a swiftly moving insect which was covered with stiff bristly hairs. It kept darting this way and that, around and around the bottom of a pit. Its gyrations made Craig a little dizzy, but he had sense enough to grab hold of a handful of hair and hang on, and as soon as his head cleared a little, he saw that the creature upon which he was now astride was pursuing Nosy.

Nosy was actually jumping, something which Craig had

never realized an ant could do. She jumped this way, then that, and each time the ant lion lunged after her. With every lunge it made a sharp cracking noise, which Craig soon realized was the snapping together of his steed's great scissorlike jaws. The ant lion was determined to make an end to Nosy, and since there was no time for the scout to clamber out of the funnellike pit, and no place to hide, that end was only a matter of time.

Craig clung tightly to his handful of bristly hair, and tried to think what he could do. He couldn't capture or subdue the ant lion. He would have to kill it, and he had only one weapon. It was hard to get the knife from his pocket while he was being jerked about so violently, and even harder to get it open, for that required two hands. But he could see that Nosy was growing tired. Her jumps didn't carry her quite so far, and the cruel jaws were coming closer each time.

Finally, Craig took a chance on falling off, and by grinding the heels of his shoes hard into the ant lion's sides, he dared release his hold on the hair long enough to open the longest blade. The next moment he plunged it into the tawny, outstretched neck.

For a moment nothing at all happened. The ant lion kept on as before, and this time the open jaws were sure to close over an exhausted Nosy. Then, without warning, the creature simply collapsed on the ground. It was as though someone had pricked a balloon, and the air had all rushed out at once. Craig found his feet resting on the sandy bottom of the pit, and he was staring down on the ant lion who no longer looked either terrifying or ferocious. Now it was nothing but a fat, rather comical insect.

"You saved me," panted Nosy, staggering over weakly to stand on trembling legs beside Craig. "You saved me from breaking the law. The ant lion would certainly have eaten me if you hadn't killed him first. They always do. Doubtless I'm the only ant who ever came out of an ant lion's pit alive. I am very grateful."

"That's all right," said Craig. He felt a little embarrassed at the way the three white eyes were looking at him.

"Perhaps," continued Nosy thoughtfully, "I was wrong in saying you couldn't be a scout."

"But I can't smell things the way you can."

"True," agreed Nosy, waggling her antennae thoughtfully. "You would probably be a better soldier, but I'd hate to have you lost in the ranks. After what has just happened, I feel responsible for you. Perhaps Her Majesty would consider allowing you to be a scout's aide."

"You mean, work with you?" cried Craig eagerly. "Oh, I'd like that. Until I get back to my regular size, I mean."

"I don't see why you should want to do that," said Nosy frankly. "It's much more satisfactory to be an ant."

"It's something I just can't explain, I guess," admitted Craig.

84

"Don't try then," advised Nosy cheerfully. "It's better to try something you know you can do than to waste your time attempting something you know you can't. Come along. Let's go back to the City, and see if Her Majesty will grant us an audience."

7

WHEN JILL RETURNED from the pasture with the eight nannies, they were immediately surrounded by the nurses who had remained behind. For a moment, the care of the eggs, the larvae and the pupae seemed to be forgotten, as, with waving antennae, the stay-at-homes made their demands known.

"We're thirsty! We've been working hard while you were out in the world filling your stomachs and crops. Give us something to drink. Divide! Divide!"

Jill tried to step back out of their way, but the little group which had singled her out followed persistently, their antennae beating demanding tattoos on her head and arms. In desperation, she looked around for Nannie, but Nannie and the other nurses were being besieged in a similar manner. They, however, were accepting the situation quite calmly. Instead of pulling back they were moving from one to another of the workers, and it seemed to Jill that they were exchanging kisses.

Then, as though she had had quite enough, Nannie brought

the proceedings to a close. Her head lifted sternly, and her antennae bristled in such a manner that the line of nurses fell back. Only those who had been confronting Jill remained unsatisfied, and they ran to Nannie, clustering about her as though they might be pouring out accusations of some kind.

Before long, Nannie bustled to Jill's side.

"You are new, and perhaps you do not understand our ways," she began, her antennae playing carefully on Jill's cheek. "Our sisters tell me you refuse to share the milk you brought back from the pasture."

"Yes," agreed Jill miserably.

"Doubtless you remember that I told you the milk from that particular herd was reserved for our babies," said Nannie after a moment. "But it is proper that the nurses also share in the milk, so you may give them a little of the supply that you brought back in your crop."

"But I didn't bring any back in my crop," confessed Jill. "I don't think I even have a crop."

"Nonsense," objected Nannie impatiently. "Of course you have a crop. Why shouldn't you? Now, stop all this selfishness at once, and give these hard-working nannies some milk."

The three pearly eyes were boring relentlessly into Jill's face. They made her uncomfortable, and she ducked her head so she would not have to meet their pitiless stare. As she did so, she noticed the slight bulge in both her pockets, and her heart gave a happy bump.

"I didn't bring back any milk in my crop," she confessed, looking once more at Nannie. "But I did bring back some of the cows, so the nurses can get their own."

She bent over and carefully emptied her pockets. One after another, she placed six little green aphids on the floor of the nursery, where they immediately, but without success, tried to extract juices from the pounded earth.

It was a long time before Nannie spoke. Her white eyes

stared at the green insects, and her antennae grew limp with shock. Finally she recovered herself.

"You brought six cows back with you? How did you carry them?"

"In my pockets," explained Jill, showing her. "Three cows exactly fill each pocket. You see, I wanted to save them from the ladybug. She was eating them so fast."

A shudder ran through Nannie's fat body.

"It was the cowgirls' problem to save the herd," she said finally. "Nurses never, never touch the cows, except to milk them. And we certainly can't have cows in the nursery."

"I'm sorry," said Jill unhappily. She reached over and began returning the little aphids to her pockets, where they would be out of sight.

"You have so much to learn," mourned Nannie. "I'm certainly beginning to see why they never trusted you with babies. Well, there's only one thing to be done. They must be returned to the stables. And since I can't be expected to handle them, you'll have to carry them."

She bounced out of the nursery, and Jill, feeling rather foolish, trotted after her. She didn't see what she had done that was so terribly wrong, but clearly Nannie was upset with her.

She had supposed that the stables would be contained in one of the small rooms off the tunnel, but to her surprise Nannie returned to the Great Hall, which she crossed and then left again through an archway on the opposite side. It was not far from where Cricket was standing, and as soon as he saw Jill coming he raised his wings and filled the room with noise.

"Hello, Jill Dear," he called enthusiastically. "I'm glad to see you back. Did you convince them that you were no good at tending babies? Are they going to let you stay with me and enjoy the music?"

"I don't know," confessed Jill uncertainly. She hoped that Nannie wouldn't get too far ahead, but it would have been impolite not to stop and exchange a few words with Cricket. "We're on our way to the stables."

"Really?" said Cricket. "I thought, when I saw Nannie coming, that it was the hour to take the larvae outside for their airing. The nurses pass by here every evening with the ugly little things. What are you going to do at the stables?"

"Return some cows," explained Jill.

"Cows? Cows?" repeated Cricket, waving his antennae questioningly.

But Jill never had an opportunity to explain, for Nannie reappeared in the archway and beckoned her on imperiously.

Like the main entrance to the Great Hall, this doorway led to a ramp, but it was steeper and not nearly so long as the one by which the children had entered the City. Moreover, it was not so dark as the main tunnel, but was illuminated by a filtered greenish light. A few doorways opened into rooms on either side, and when Nannie turned off into one of them, Jill followed.

They were in a dome-shaped chamber which must have been quite close to the ground, for light was sifting through a matted tangle of dried reeds and grasses in the roof. Short lengths of small branches and piles of wilting leaves were scattered around the room, and in the very center a dozen or more ants had gathered in an open circle. They did not look up as Nannie and Jill entered. In fact, they gave no indication that they were even aware of visitors.

"Come," said Nannie, touching Jill in surprise. "Something is clearly wrong here. Let's see what it's all about."

Jill stayed close beside her as Nannie advanced to the circle. The ants were sitting close together with bent heads and sadly waving antennae. From time to time, one of them touched the sensitive feelers of the insect next to her who, in turn, touched her sister on the other side, and so on until every ant in the circle had been contacted.

"Why," said Jill in pleased recognition. "We used to play that game at parties. Somebody whispers something to the next person, and he whispers it to the next, and it goes on around the room. Only it never comes out the way it started."

"Stop communicating," ordered Nannie. "Let's push our way in here, and see what the conference is about."

For the moment, she seemed to have forgotten the errand which had brought them to the stables, a fact which Jill found very gratifying. She didn't like Nannie to be angry with her.

The ants gave way reluctantly, but Nannie's strong forelegs were insistent. She pushed and wedged and wriggled until the circle had widened enough to include herself and Jill. Thereupon she settled down to learn what problem was under discussion. It was not long before one of the comments reached them. Jill received it from the cowgirl on her right, and obediently passed it on to Nannie on her left.

"This is the greatest misfortune that has ever befallen the City."

Nannie's antennae shrugged with uncomprehension, and she changed the message just a little as she passed it on.

"What is the greatest misfortune which has ever befallen the City?"

By the time the communication had run around the circle and reached Jill, it was changed back to the way it was the first time.

"Why, *this* is the greatest misfortune which has ever befallen the City!"

At once Nannie lost all patience. She pranced out into the center of the ring where they could all see her, and brandished her antennae fiercely before returning to her place. This time it was she who started the questioning.

"I am Nannie, one of the head nurses in charge of the royal babies. I am here on important business, and I demand to know why you herders of cows are sitting around wasting time instead of working at your occupation as you should be."

Her criticism must have stung their pride, for after that the replies came from both sides, and so fast that Jill could hardly keep up with them.

"This is a needful council, and you will be one of the first to agree to that, Nannie, when you hear what has happened."

"Tell me quickly," she ordered. "I, too, am probably wasting time while I stop to listen."

"The royal herd, the one which was fed on rose leaves and

was kept for the exclusive use of the nursery, has been completely wiped out! First there was a ladybug, and even before she was gone two aphid-wolves descended upon it. Our herders could do nothing! Every one of those prize cows that we raised so carefully is gone. There's not even a start for a new herd."

"No, they're not," cried Jill, before Nannie had a chance to reply. She jumped up and carefully unloaded the contents of her pinafore pocket, placing the six little aphids down in the center of the ring.

Immediately the cowgirls broke their circle to advance upon their charges, snatching them up and petting them fondly.

"Well, well," sputtered Nannie, and Jill had the impression that she was a little embarrassed. "Perhaps, under the circumstances it's just as well that you brought the cows along. But I must say, I've never before heard of anyone who had a carrying-bag built right into her skin as you do. Mashers are certainly oddly made creatures."

"This isn't my skin. It's my pinafore," explained Jill. "And pinafores always have pockets. You can carry all sorts of things in them. You can even carry more than that if you hold them in the skirt this way."

"I do believe you can," marveled Nannie. "That's going to be very practical when it comes time to take the babies out for their airing. You can transport a goodly number at one time."

The cowgirls had carried their six charges to one of the green branches against the wall, and already the aphids had settled down to graze. Now the herders were back, crowding around Jill, and one of them touched the little girl delicately with her antennae.

"You are a heroine," she praised. "We insist that you stay here in the stables with us always, and help us look after our beautiful cows. Perhaps, in time, we will be able to show you how grateful we are."

"Nonsense," objected Nannie angrily. "Why should she want to stay here and tend cows? She wants to work in the nursery with us, and take care of the babies."

"But we are so grateful to you," insisted the cowgirl, ignoring Nannie and stroking Jill softly. "I know you will be happy with us. You have already proved how successful you could be in our work. We want you to stay. I, myself, will go to the queen and request permission that you be transferred."

"Then I shall go to the queen and insist that she remain in the nursery!" Nannie's fat little body shook with rage. "I didn't know before that she had those carrying bags in her skin. I can see lots of opportunity for her in the nursery, and I don't intend that she shall be demoted to the stable."

"Demoted!" The cowgirl drew herself up indignantly. "Without us to supply the formulae, where would your precious nursery be, I'd like to know? Demoted indeed!"

"Yes, demoted," repeated Nannie stubbornly. "Honeydew is not the only food, remember. It's not mentioned by name in the law, but babies are!"

"Nevertheless, I shall speak to the queen." The cowgirl patted Jill gently. "Come, dear heroine. We will go to see Her Majesty right now."

"Not without me, she doesn't," protested Nannie, and she locked her right foreleg firmly around Jill's left arm. The cowgirl circled to the other side, and just as resolutely took Jill's right arm, and pulling her between them, they galloped out of the stables.

Jill had never run so fast before in her life, for the ants on either side hurried her over the ground so rapidly that often her feet did not touch at all. Cricket called to her cheerfully as she was whisked by him in the Great Hall, but she had neither time nor breath to answer. Almost before she knew it, they were back in the opposite tunnel, and had pulled up before a door where someone was blocking the way. Jill shook her head to push back a lock of hair which had blown down into her eyes, and saw that the someone was My Lady.

"Such unseemly haste!" disapproved the queen's lady in waiting. "And why have you brought the Masher here? Her Majesty ordered you to put her to work."

"I want to do just that, My Lady," the cowgirl insisted earnestly. "We want her in the stables. She's a heroine. She saved the rose-cows from extinction, and I'm here to beg Her Majesty to give her to us."

"Which is quite ridiculous, of course," bristled Nannie, "since she's already been given to us, and is working out quite well."

"Of the two Mashers, she did have the greatest possibilities," admitted My Lady. "But I'm not sure that Her Majesty should be disturbed right now. She's exhausted from her egg laying, and she's being bathed."

"Then there's no need to disturb her at all," decided Nannie. "We'll just go right back to the nursery where we belong."

"No, we won't!" The cowgirl was most stubborn. "Please request Her Majesty to grant us an audience, My Lady. It's very important. This—this"—she glanced at Jill uncertainly, not exactly sure what to call her—"this new resident of the City could be the greatest boon which the dairy industry has ever known. Please ask the queen to see us."

"Very well," agreed My Lady, after a moment. "I'll present your request."

She disappeared into the room, and the three of them stood waiting.

"I'm sure the queen will agree that you should come with us." The cowgirl's antennae barely stirred, but Nannie on the other side of Jill, managed to pick up the communication.

"Her Majesty is no fool! Or she wouldn't be Her Majesty. Naturally she'll command that you remain in the nursery," said Nannie scornfully.

94

My Lady was gone for some time, but at last she returned with the information that the queen would see them.

"But only for a minute," she warned sternly. "The royal bath is finished, and Her Majesty is being brushed. After that she will continue with her duties. You mustn't stay long enough to interfere with that."

She ushered them inside, then, with a deep curtsy, fell back and left them standing alone.

Unlike her mother's, the young queen's body was not dull with age. It fairly glittered, and two maids, one on either side, were adding to that sheen by polishing it with the long combs on their forelegs. Her regal head was held high, her antennae straight and unbending, and it seemed to Jill that there was even an imperial flash to the three royal white eyes which regarded the visitors.

Nannie and the cowgirl bent their front legs in a curtsy, and Jill found herself bowing also. It was, apparently, the correct thing to do, and after a moment one of the royal antennae beckoned them to approach.

"So you are one of the Mashers I was forced to reduce to its proper stature," said the queen coldly. "You called me a bug!"

Jill felt the eyes of the cowgirl and Nannie boring into her face, and their grasps on her arms tightened accusingly.

"I'm sorry, Your Majesty," she quavered. "Was—was that wrong?"

"Certainly, stupid! All insects are not bugs. There is a difference. If I were a cinch bug or a squash bug, or one of their cousins, you would be correct. They are true bugs. But I am not one of them. If I had wings which folded flat over my back, and a beak with which I could suck plant juices or animal blood you might call me a bug. But do you see such a beak on me?"

"No, Your Majesty."

"Of course not!" The queen turned her body slightly in order

95

to give them a better view of the imperial profile. One of the maids, who had been working on her left side, was swept off her feet by this sudden move, and for a moment disappeared completely under the huge, glistening abdomen of her mistress. A moment later she managed to wriggle out from under, and fell to polishing once more with as much zeal as ever.

"Well, why are you here?" demanded the queen, after a moment. "You have heard the crime. You know the punishment. What more is there to be said?"

"Your Majesty," began the cowgirl humbly. "I did not know before that she was a—a Masher, or guilty of so terrible a crime, but Your Majesty, she has accomplished a heroic deed. I came to beg that she might be turned over to the workers in the stable, where she would be able to repeat these services to the City."

"Your Majesty, such a decree would be unwise," interrupted Nannie. "The prisoner has been assigned to the nursery. Rest assured that we will be able to put her accomplishment to good use where she is, now that we know she has this ability."

"Just what did the Masher do which was of such merit?" demanded the queen haughtily.

"Your Majesty, she saved the herd of rose-cows," explained the cowgirl quickly. "As you know, we now have only one herd of this kind. We have many herds of apple aphids and cherry aphids, and of the varieties which thrive on small flowering plants. But the rose-cow herd was just being built up. It was doing so well, too. And without this—Masher, we would have lost them all."

"If you herders had been alert——" began Nannie, but fell silent at a warning twitch of the royal antennae.

"How many rose-cows did the Masher save?" asked the queen.

For a moment the cowgirl seemed lost in thought. Her antennae moved rapidly, as though they might be adding up a score.

"Two million, one hundred and sixty thousand cows, Your Majesty," she answered finally.

Jill gave a gasp of astonishment. It was flattering to know that they both wanted her help, but it certainly wasn't right to lie about things.

"I only brought back six aphids, Your Majesty," she corrected.

"Exactly," agreed the cowgirl calmly. "I'm not very good at numbers, but I believe that's the way it comes out. Six cows will have 200 babies each. That's 1200 cows to start with. There will be nine generations a year, which makes 10,800. Multiply that by the 200 babies, and we get 2,160,000. That is the number of rose-cows which the Masher saved for us today. And, of course, that's only the beginning. It goes on and on."

"Your Majesty," interrupted Nannie hastily. "You know how important it is that the larvae take the air each evening. And there's always the problem of transporting eggs from one nursery to another as the temperature changes, and of carrying the pupae to the Delivery Room. Oh, there's always a transportation problem in the nursery."

"That is so," agreed the queen.

"Now the reason she was able to save the cows," continued Nannie, glaring from her side eye at the cowgirl, "is that Mashers have carrying bags in their skins. Instead of transporting one object at a time, she was able to carry six, three in each bag. Now I understand she can carry even more. Consider, Your Majesty, what a timesaver that would be in our busy nursery. I feel that she should stay where she is."

"But we need her, Your Majesty," insisted the cowgirl. "Think of our constant war with the enemies of our cows—the aphid lions, the aphid wolves, the ladybugs——"

"So do we need her," snapped Nannie. "And she was given to us first!"

"Cease!" The queen's antennae shook with indignation. "You are quarreling among yourselves, you who are sisters! It was my mistake in bringing the Masher here in the first place. She is the cause of the dissension, and she will have to leave."

"Then please let me go home, Your Majesty," pleaded Jill. "Change me, and Craig too, back to the way we were."

"Oh, yes," remembered the queen. "There were two of you. What has happened to the other Masher?"

"He was a male, Your Majesty." My Lady stepped forward, her sleek body shuddering a little at the repugnance of the idea. "So he's worth nothing at all. I set him to work with the engineers, but he won't be able to do his share. He hasn't even returned from carrying out his first load."

"Let me have a report when he does," decided the queen. "If he is worth nothing, and the girl is a troublemaker, we'd better just send them both home."

"Oh, thank you. Thank you," cried Jill joyfully.

"In the meantime," continued Her Majesty, as though she had not even heard, "she might as well continue on in the nursery. It would be better not to have her out in one of the pastures where we can't find her again when it comes time to change her back."

8

It WAS MUCH EASIER for Craig to travel with Nosy than it had been with the other ants.

"Since you're only going to be a scout's aide, not a true scout, you won't be expected to cover all the territory I do," Nosy had informed him as they climbed out of the ant lion's pit and started down the path. "I'll just point you in the right direction, and you continue on a straight course. I'll make all the necessary side trips, and catch up with you from time to time."

It really worked out very well. Nosy's journey back to the City took her in a zigzag route. She explored both sides of the path, often disappearing for a time into the concealing growth at the edge, but she always returned to Craig, slowing her steps momentarily while they exchanged a few comments.

"Mashers have been around here," she informed him sadly as they neared the steps. "I just encountered two of our sisters who were completely crushed. There's hardly enough of them to carry home for a proper burial."

"You mean you bring dead ants back to the City and hold funerals?" asked Craig in amazement.

"It's the only decent thing to do," Nosy told him primly. "After all, they didn't break the law. They weren't eaten. Where do Mashers put their dead?"

"In cemeteries, of course."

"So do we," pointed out Nosy triumphantly. "It's getting dark, and we'd better hurry and tell the undertakers, so they can come for the bodies."

"I suppose we could take them back ourselves," suggested Craig a little reluctantly.

"I thought you wanted to be a scout!" Nosy's antennae twitched impatiently. "Scouts seek things out and sound alarms. We haven't time to stop and carry heavy burdens."

"Oh," said Craig. More than ever he was glad that he was going to serve as Nosy's aide.

Since there was nothing to scout for in the tunnel, Nosy did not make side excursions, and she reached the Great Hall far ahead of Craig. He was a little afraid that he might be challenged by the sentinels at the door, but they let him pass into the vanilla-scented room. Immediately Nosy was at his side.

"This way," she told him. "I've already notified the undertakers, and they're on their way. So that's been taken care of. Now the masseurs are waiting for us."

"Masseurs?"

"Certainly. I'm a little stiff from all that jumping I did to avoid the ant lion, and you must be tired, too. Besides, we're both dirty. A bath and a good massage, and I promise we'll feel better. After that I must see the queen about your appointment."

Nosy hurried him to a corner where four ants were waiting. As soon as they arrived, two of them grasped Craig with strong forelegs, threw him to the floor, and began to pound and massage his back. They caught him unaware, and for a moment he tried to fight back. Then he saw that Nosy was being treated in a similar fashion by the other two ants, and didn't appear to resent it at all. Craig decided that he was expected to lie still, and after a moment the rubbing and massaging on his tired muscles began to feel very relaxing.

"Who are you?" he gasped, addressing one of the ants. By this time he had been flipped over on his back, and they were kneading the upper parts of his arms.

"I am Rubber," the ant told him briefly.

"Do you do this all the time?"

"It's my job," said Rubber. "I do other things as they are required, but this is my specialty. I must say, you have a peculiar kind of skin. It doesn't stick to you."

She lifted a fold of Craig's tee-shirt and held it out disapprovingly.

"That's not my skin. It's my clothes," explained Craig. "I can take them off."

"Ah," said Rubber with understanding. "You're one of those insects which sheds its skin. I wonder what you'll be when you discard this one."

"I'll be the same as I am now," insisted Craig. "I won't change."

"Of course you'll change," said Rubber. "You never know, poor things, what you'll be next. It's always a great surprise to you."

The masseurs left off rubbing, and now began to wash their two clients, using their quick little tongues for the purpose. Craig shut his eyes while this was going on. He didn't like the idea of being licked by an ant, but he was afraid to protest; they might not understand. After a moment, he decided that so long as he didn't have to watch, the washing wasn't so bad. He could pretend that the rough tongue was a warm terrycloth washrag, one which was scented with vanilla soap.

Following the bath, Nosy and Craig were carefully combed with the edges of the masseurs' front legs. Craig did not feel that this step amounted to much, especially so far as he was concerned. The combs kept catching on tiny threads of his clothing, and Rubber had to pause and get them untangled. And while they might have imparted a polish to Nosy's hard black coat, they had no effect at all on Craig's skin or clothing.

At last the scout pushed herself free of the busily polishing feet.

"Enough of this," she cried. "If you overdo it, they'll mistake me for My Lady. Come along, Craig. Let's see what the grubbers brought in for dinner."

Craig's heart sank with remembrance.

"I'm afraid it was that slug."

"Of course," recalled Nosy in delight. "There's nothing so hearty and sustaining as meat. The buffet will be in the center of the hall."

The gray slug was, indeed, the evening's meal, and already most of it had disappeared. The portion remaining was so small that it now had the appearance of a pork roast. From time to time, one of the ants approached, snipped off a small fragment, then hurried away to resume whatever work had occupied her before.

"Help yourself," invited Nosy, waving a hospitable antenna.

"I—I don't think I'm hungry," gulped Craig.

Nosy grew stern.

"If you don't eat, you can't keep up your strength. And if you aren't strong, you can't be a scout's aide. Eat, or I'll send you back to the engineers."

The threat was enough. Craig couldn't go back to hauling dirt in the company of those who obviously didn't even care whether he was around. If he had to remain with the ants he wanted to be with one who liked him, one who would take the trouble to talk and explain things. He bent over the pale gray meat and opened his mouth slightly, trying to pretend that it was pork. He had forgotten that it was so soft, and his teeth went farther than he intended. When he stood up, his mouth was completely filled.

"That's better," approved Nosy, and bent her own head. A moment later she straightened up, gulped once, and stood waiting patiently for Craig to swallow.

He chewed as fast as he could, marveling that the slug didn't make him sick, but it didn't have that effect at all. It had a meaty flavor, although the texture was rather like jelly. He decided that it wasn't bad at all, and almost immediately his stomach began to feel full.

"What in the world are you doing?" demanded Nosy curiously. Her three white eyes had been following every movement of his jaws.

"Just chewing." He swallowed the last bit. "Didn't you chew yours at all? Did you swallow it whole?"

"Naturally not," said Nosy in surprise. "Ants never swallow anything but liquids. It's still in my mouth, where the juices are being extracted. I'll swallow them, and part will go to my stomach, part to my crop for the use of my friends."

"And what will you do with the part that isn't liquid?"

"Spit it out, naturally. The garbage collectors will come along and carry it outside. Or we could walk over and give it to Cricket. He's always so grateful for an extra tidbit."

"Oh, let's do," agreed Craig eagerly. "I like Cricket."

Cricket was delighted to see them, and as Nosy had said, grateful for the solid bits of slug which the scout deposited at his feet.

"Didn't you remember me, too, Cousin Craig?" asked Cricket reproachfully. "Don't tell me you threw away good food without even a thought for your old friend?"

103

"I'm afraid I swallowed mine," confessed Craig. "But I could run back and bring you a fresh piece."

"You'd better not," advised Nosy. "It might be misunderstood by those whose special job it is to feed the pets."

"Pet," corrected Cricket sadly. "There used to be more of us. Spider was here for a time, and there were several beetles. But now there's only I."

"You're quite enough," Nosy told him hastily. "Will you entertain Craig while I go to the queen to ask a favor? I want Her Majesty to release Craig from the engineers and assign her to me as an aide."

Cricket's sharp black eyes glittered, and his stiff antennae stood upright in alarm.

"You mustn't even consider such a thing," he protested. "That wouldn't be suitable at all. Do you realize that Cousin Craig is a boy?"

Craig looked at Cricket indignantly. Why was he trying to spoil things, anyway? He had been the one to advise against mentioning Craig's sex, and now here he was bringing it up. The subject had not been mentioned by Nosy before, and she must have taken it for granted that Craig was a girl.

"Really?" Nosy's antennae trembled a little, but she did not draw back as My Lady had done. "In that case, perhaps I would be wasting my time in making such a request. Craig will not even be alive tomorrow. Males live only a single day."

"Cricket's a boy, and he's lived more than one day," pointed out Craig. "And so do Mashers. It's only ants that have such a silly custom."

"It isn't silly at all," argued Nosy mildly. "Males serve their purpose in a day. There's nothing more for them to do."

"Well, there's lots of things for me to do," insisted Craig. "If I'd only lived one day I wouldn't have been here to save you from the ant lion, would I?"

"What's this? What's this?" demanded Cricket.

"This Masher has a secret weapon," explained Nosy. "He carries a hidden stinger in a little bag. He can take it out when he pleases, and his enemy drops dead. I was captured by an ant lion, and he rescued me."

"A hidden weapon?" repeated Cricket. "I didn't know about that, Cousin Craig. I didn't know that you could protect yourself against your enemies. A scout runs into all kinds of danger. I didn't want you to be hurt. I wanted you to stay here, where you'd be safe."

"It's a knife," explained Craig, pulling it from his pocket and opening it to show them.

"It looks hurty," shuddered Cricket. "Put it back in your skin."

"How long do the males live among you Mashers?" asked Nosy curiously.

"As long as the ladies do. Years and years," Craig assured her. "Unless, of course, they get terribly sick, or have an accident."

"Those things can happen to us, too," agreed Nosy. "And how are you treated by the women? Do they tolerate you?"

"I should say so," sputtered Craig angrily. "They—they——"

"Careful, careful," warned Cricket, placing a restraining leg over his shoulders.

"Yes, they do," said Craig after a moment, realizing that Cricket was right and that he mustn't say anything which might offend the scout. "They like us very much. They're always glad when we're around."

"In that case," decided Nosy, "perhaps I, too, should be big about this matter. I'll overlook your misfortune, and go ahead with our original plan. I'll go to see Her Majesty at once."

She turned and hurried away across the Great Hall, and Craig reached up and patted the hard leg across his shoulders. He was no longer angry with Cricket, who had only been trying to save him from possible danger.

Cricket looked back at him mournfully. In spite of the secret weapon, he knew that the life of a scout's aide would be filled with peril. His stiff antennae wobbled with emotion, and the wings, folded neatly over his back, wavered a little at the edges.

"Why don't you give us a little music?" suggested Craig impulsively. "It will help pass the time while we're waiting."

"Delighted," replied Cricket instantly, and the sorrow faded from his eyes as he lifted his wings.

The crick, crick, crick, so close to his ears, was deafening, and almost more than Craig could stand. Once or twice it seemed that Cricket was getting tired, for the cricks grew slower, the pauses between, a little longer. But every time Craig looked up hopefully, Cricket seemed to receive a new burst of enthusiasm and the tempo increased. It was better, Craig decided, not to look at Cricket at all, so instead he glanced around the Great Hall at the unceasing industry on every hand, and marveled that the ants weren't exhausted. It must be completely dark outside by this time, yet not one seemed to be wearing down. He remembered what Nosy had told him about ants sleeping all winter, and wondered if they stayed awake all summer to make up for it.

Suddenly he was aware of a line of ants hurrying past him, who disappeared through an archway in the wall beside Cricket. Each seemed to be carrying something in her mouth, and while he was trying to decide what it could be, Cricket stopped his music abruptly.

"It's night outside," he observed cheerfully. "There go the nannies with the larvae. They take them out every evening after the sun goes down for an airing. The day's heat is much too drying on a larva's sensitive skin, you know."

"Is that so?" asked Craig politely.

"Yes, indeed," Cricket assured him. "Now we must both watch sharp and call to Jill Dear as she goes by. She's helping in the nursery, and they're sure to put her to airing the larvae."

"Are you sure?" cried Craig, but even as he spoke he saw his cousin approaching across the floor.

She was walking as fast as she could, and holding her sagging pinafore out in front of her. On either side, little nursemaids danced along, slowing their steps to match hers.

"Jill!" cried Craig eagerly. "Jill! Over here!"

She looked up and saw him. Immediately she began running, and the nursemaids jiggled with anxiety. Clearly they were afraid she might fall and spill whatever she carried.

"Oh, Craig," Jill cried. "How are you? Have you been getting along all right? I've been so worried."

"Fine! I'm going to be a scout's aide," he shouted. "What have you got in your apron?"

"Larvae," she told him as she reached the corner. "At first I was going to carry them in my pocket, but I made the mistake of showing Nannie how many more my pinafore would hold."

"That was unfortunate," said Cricket sadly. "From now on you'll have to work, work, work. You'll have no time to enjoy music at all."

"No, I won't," denied Jill quickly. "Because the queen's going to change us back. At least, she's thinking about it. She was only waiting till you got back to decide, Craig. I made dissension, and she says you're of no use because you're a boy."

"What do you mean, dissension?" asked Cricket, but Craig interrupted indignantly.

"I am, too, of use. Ask Nosy."

"Well, it will all be over before long." Jill had to shout her last remarks over her shoulder, for the nursemaids, impatient at her delay, had picked her up and were carrying her away. "We'll be home soon. Probably in an hour or so."

"I hope she's right." Craig watched her disappear through the archway. "I'll be awfully glad to get out of this place."

"Oh, there are worse spots," insisted Cricket cheerfully. "But at least you won't have to run the dangers of being a scout's aide. In spite of your hidden weapon, I'd be quite nervous thinking of you as a scout, Cousin Craig."

"Nosy will be disappointed," said Craig. "I hate to let her down, and when the queen tells her we're to go home I'm afraid she'll feel pretty sad."

But when Nosy finally appeared, she did not look sad. She frisked along, her antennae tilted rakishly, and as she crossed the Great Hall she paused more than once to disrupt the labors of a working ant by a playful poke with one of her wiry legs.

"I did it," she boasted, coming up before them and prodding

them each in turn. "I had a time, too. More than once I thought Her Majesty was going to have me thrown out, but I finally wore her down."

"You did what, Nosy?" It was Cricket who asked the question, for Craig was already beginning to guess the cause of Nosy's exuberance, and was close to tears.

"What I set out to do, of course," said Nosy. "Craig's going to be my scout's aide. I had a bad time convincing Her Majesty that he was worth keeping at all, but she finally saw it my way. You see, some other Masher arrived at the same time as Craig, and she's stirred up a lot of trouble. The queen was about ready to turn them both loose, but now she's going to give them another chance."

•

9

CRAIG WAS AWAKENED by something tickling his cheek, and for a moment he thought he was in his own bed and that Bones, his Boston terrier, was pawing gently, telling him that it was time to get up and go outside to play. Then he heard someone speaking to him, and knew that it wasn't Bones at all, for Bones had to depend on sign language to make his wants known.

"Certainly this should be enough rest for anyone. It's still summer, and if you sleep it all away what are you going to do in winter when there's no one else awake, and nothing at all to eat?"

He opened his eyes, and there was Nosy, prodding him disapprovingly. Over the scout's shoulder he caught a glimpse of Cricket's sympathetic eyes and bristling antennae, and Craig realized, with a great surge of despair, that he hadn't been dreaming. He was still in the City Under the Back Steps, and was expected to serve as a scout's aide.

He forgot that for a time he had actually wanted to help Nosy, and that she was the only ant who had seemed at all friendly toward him. Now he felt only resentment toward the wiry little scout. If it hadn't been for her, Jill and he would be home by this time, safely restored to their natural sizes.

He had told her over and over that he didn't want to be an ant, that he wanted to be a human being, but for some reason Nosy couldn't understand. She actually seemed to feel that she had done him a favor by keeping him here. Craig had argued and shouted, threatened and finally cried, all to no avail. Nosy had been very interested in the tears, and had even tasted one of them, but she had stubbornly refused to revisit the queen and ask that Craig and Jill be released.

Craig had appealed to Cricket for support, but Cricket declined to take sides. He had patted the boy comfortingly, and when Craig, exhausted from his day's work, had dropped off to sleep in the middle of the discussion, Cricket had convinced the scout that the boy should be left alone for a while. But now Nosy was back and impatiently calling for her new assistant.

Craig stood up. Despite the efforts of the masseurs, his muscles ached from the unusual amount of walking and carrying he had done yesterday.

"Breakfast?" asked Nosy brightly. Her face pressed close to his, and under the force of those three commanding eyes, Craig obediently opened his mouth. It was filled with warm, sweet liquid which seemed to revive him instantly.

"The sun is coming up, and it's time to scout the Cinnamon City of the enemy," announced Nosy. She seemed determined to overlook their argument of last night, and to start the day as though nothing had happened.

Perhaps it was just as well, Craig told himself. It would be better to keep on friendly relations with Nosy if he had to face the outer world in his present size. But somehow he must convince the scout that she was wrong, that he wasn't the help she had expected him to be. If he did that, she might be willing to admit her mistake to the queen, and he and Jill would be released.

"I'm ready," he assured her. Then turning to Cricket, "If you see Jill, tell her I'll think of a plan. Tell her not to give up hope."

"I'm not likely to see her again until evening," said Cricket. "They'll keep her busy in the nurseries all day. But you be careful, Cousin Craig. The outside world is very dangerous."

When they walked out of the darkness under the bottom step, Craig thought that someone must have changed the tunnel during the night so that it led out into a strange world, not the familiar one. Everything sparkled with every color in the rainbow. There were the cool blues and greens of opals, the fiery reds of rubies, the yellows of topaz, and the deep, glowing richness of amethyst. Under the rays of the early sun, the glittering gems shimmered and danced on the green fronds of the waving grass overhead, and dotted the rough brown earth underfoot. It was as though some giant had ruthlessly scattered the contents of a jewel box about, then gone away and left them.

"What is it?" he gasped weakly.

"Dew," said Nosy. "Drink a little, if you care for it. But don't take too long. We've quite a way to go to the hydrangea bush."

Craig stepped close to one of the great shimmering drops, and bent his head. Never had anything tasted so fresh and delicious. Compared with this, all the water he had ever drunk before was flat and insipid.

But he began to change his opinion about the virtues of dew as they went along. They traveled a new trail, one which Nosy explained was so seldom used that it was beginning to close over. From time to time they had to push the stalks to one side in order to push through, and whenever they did a shower

of cold water cascaded down upon them. It fell harmlessly from
Nosy's black oiled coat to the ground, but Craig was immediately wet through. Rivulets dripped from his hair down his
face and neck. His tee-shirt clung damply to his back, and his
feet sloshed up and down in his soggy shoes. Since the grass
tops overhead kept the sun from striking his body, there was
no opportunity to dry out, and before long goose bumps covered his arms, and his teeth were chattering.

"What are you doing now?" demanded Nosy, pushing aside

dripping blades to rejoin him after one of her scouting trips to the side. "Your skin is swelling, and your teeth are rattling as though they wanted to bite somebody. Is this one of the customs of the Mashers?"

"It's because I'm cold," explained Craig, frowning. "It's wet down here. Let's get out in the sun."

"You should be glad of the cold," reproved Nosy. "Ants always run slower when it's cold, and faster when it's hot. Since you can't smell your own way, you have less trouble keeping up with me now. You don't want to get lost on a dim trail, do you?"

"No, I don't," admitted Craig.

"From now on we must be very careful," cautioned Nosy. "I'm beginning to get the scent of cinnamon, which means that the wind is in our favor. The red ants' city is just ahead."

"What are we going to do when we get there?" asked Craig, stifling a sneeze.

"Spy on them. Make sure they aren't up to anything," said Nosy. "It's part of my job."

"Isn't it dangerous?"

"Of course," agreed Nosy casually. "Isn't everything?"

"What I mean is, what would they do with you if they caught you?"

"Oh, I'd be beheaded immediately, and probably eaten. But I'm no lawbreaker. So I don't intend that to happen."

"I'm glad you don't," said Craig.

"There's really not so much danger today of being discovered," continued Nosy. "A new mountain has just erupted a short distance from the entrance to the Cinnamon City. We can climb to the top of it, and look down. Unless, of course, the Mashers have taken it into their heads to flatten the mountain. They always do, sooner or later."

"Mountain?" repeated Craig, puzzled. Then he remembered that only yesterday his father had announced that he must set a trap for a mole which had been burrowing in the back yard.

"Yes, mountain," agreed Nosy. "You'll see it for yourself in a minute. And you'll have a chance to get warm while we're on top."

It took Craig a long time to climb to the top of the molehill when they arrived. The soft ground slid under his feet, and while it was easy enough to find footing, the soil was inclined to crumble. His clothes began to steam the moment he came out in the sunlight. It swirled about him in wisps of fog, sometimes so thick that he could hardly see ahead. Nosy began to pick up speed as soon as they stepped out of the cool shade, and she raced ahead up the steep slope which seemed to present no difficulty at all to her six legs.

Overhead the sky was blue and cloudless, and now that Craig had climbed to the same height as the grasstops, they did not look like a jungle any more. Instead they were more like a great green sea. Caressed by the wind, they rolled softly in long waves which never quite turned into white breakers.

From the vantage point of half way up the molehill, Craig could look over the whole of the back yard. There was the apple tree with his swing hanging from the lowest branch. How huge and grotesque it looked, a tree and a swing for some giant. And there was his house. The blinds were still closed downstairs, and the upper windows were open. It must be very early and his mother and father were still asleep. He wondered how they could sleep when he, their very own son, was missing. He gulped back a great lump which appeared in his throat, and blinked back tears, all the while making his feet take one step after another, and using his hands to keep himself from sliding backward.

He did not realize he had arrived at the top until he felt the rough edges of one of Nosy's strong front feet reach down and grasp his shirt firmly, pulling him up the last ascent.

"My," reproved Nosy. "You aren't much of a mountain climber, are you? I thought you'd never make it."

"I kept slipping back," puffed Craig. "I don't think I'm going to be much help to you as an aide, Nosy. I'm too slow."

"You'll work up speed as you practice," the scout assured him confidently. "And speed isn't everything. That hidden weapon of yours is pretty important, you know. Well, there's the Cinnamon City. Take a good look."

Craig's eyes followed the pointing foot. There was the hydrangea bush, its wide green leaves extended stiffly so that the sun could dry them after their morning's shower of dew, the tight little buds, which would unfold later into blue blossoms, as stiffly erect as Cricket's antennae. His eyes traveled down the brown trunk to the ground below, and stopped.

If this was an ant city, its inhabitants were certainly unlike the busy workers who lived under the back steps. There were perhaps fifty or sixty of them sitting quietly in the sun before the entrance, and doing nothing at all. Their red bodies gleamed, but not a single leg or antenna moved in industry or communication. As Craig stared in wonder at this singular spectacle of idle ants, a group of black ants emerged from a dark hole in the earth and hurried toward the red ones. As they passed along the silent line, pausing momentarily before each of the red warriors in turn, Nosy's antennae twitched with resentment.

"Who are they?" whispered Craig. "The black ones? I thought you said this was a red ant city?"

"Those are some of our sisters." Nosy's antennae throbbed angrily. "Did you not receive the whiff of vanilla when they came out of the tunnel? How it irks me to smell it blended with that harsh cinnamon."

"What are they doing here, living with the red ants?"

"They are slaves," admitted Nosy a little reluctantly. "They were taken by the red soldiers on their last raid on our city.

116

Now they must serve their mistresses. See, they are feeding them."

"Goodness," said Craig in awed surprise. "You don't have slaves, do you?"

"Certainly not," denied Nosy crossly. "We would not like to be called lazy. We do our own work. But the red ants know only warfare. They do not work at all, except perhaps to oil their armor occasionally. They keep slaves to feed them, and care for their babies, and to raise their cows, and build and take care of their city. They, themselves, do nothing."

"How many of your sisters do they have as slaves?" asked Craig, for suddenly a great stream of black workers began pouring out of the hole beside the hydrangea. There were so many of them that the red ants were completely blocked from view.

"Thousands," snapped Nosy. "In the last raid, they emptied the nursery of eggs and larvae and pupae. It was a great tragedy, losing all our babies that way. You've no idea how it aged Her Majesty. Broke her spirit. That's why she agreed to a second queen in the City. We had to make up the loss of all those children some way."

"I don't see what good it did to steal babies," puzzled Craig. "Why didn't they steal grown ants if they wanted slaves?"

"The babies became adults, didn't they?" Nosy pointed out impatiently. "It didn't take long. The nursemaid slaves took care of them, and when the children were grown they adjusted to their new life of serving their mistresses. Those workers you see out there right now are probably some of the babies the red monsters stole from us early this spring."

"I think that's dreadful," decided Craig. "Why don't they revolt?"

"What is that?" asked Nosy curiously.

"Run away. Come home."

"They never have," Nosy told him sadly. Then, with a return to her usual briskness, she added, "Well, it looks calm enough.

I don't think the red ants are planning an attack today. We might as well go home."

It was much easier descending the mountain than it had been climbing up. Craig merely sat down, gave himself a push with his feet, and slid down the entire slope. In this manner he reached the bottom before Nosy, who came hurrying up after a moment and gave him an approving glance from her white eyes.

"You see," she pointed out, "I told you that achieving speed was only a matter of practice."

But Craig paid no attention, for his ears had caught an ominous noise. First there had been a couple of dull cracks, then a great roar. A moment later a plume of blue-gray smoke drifted over the top of the grass, and his nose was filled with a familiar scent. Gasoline and oil! It added up to just one thing. Jim, the handy man, had chosen this morning to cut the lawn.

"We've got to get out of here!" Craig turned to Nosy in panic. "We'll be mowed down, maybe crushed by the roller."

"We'll be careful," agreed Nosy calmly. "We can always stay close to the edges. The Mashers never cut them until last. Come along. It's this way."

Craig followed, quaking as the sound of the power mower grew louder, and relaxing a little as it faded when Jim turned backward on the row. This time he did not need Nosy to encourage him to greater speed. He ran as fast as his legs would carry him, picking himself up whenever a foot got tangled over a grassblade, and hurrying over a trail that was even dimmer than the one they had followed earlier. Only when they reached the petunias at the property line did he relax a little and pause to get his breath. Almost immediately Nosy came hurrying back for him.

"Success!" she cried. "I've found a second breakfast for us, and beat the grubbers out besides. They won't be on to this catch for hours, and by the time they find it and return to the City for help, the Masher may have moved it!"

"What is it?" panted Craig, but Nosy only waggled her antennae and darted away along the petunias.

Craig had not helped dig this bed, so there were no big clods to bar the way. The spaded ground was almost smooth under his feet as he hurried after the scout. Then, without warning, his path was barred by a gigantic brown object the likes of which he had never seen.

It was as huge as a dirigible, and the sides were glassy smooth, but dull. As he peered up, he could see that it puffed out for some distance, but at the very top it was gathered into a small neck. There was no head above the neck, and the object was not alive, so Craig found courage to touch it gently with his finger. It bent and crackled just a little, and he realized it was a brown paper sack, probably containing Jim's lunch.

Nosy was climbing the perpendicular sides effortlessly, and now she turned and motioned him to follow. Craig tried, but there was nothing to which he could cling, and he couldn't be expected to climb up a flat wall. He shook his head at the scout mournfully, and after a moment Nosy scampered down to him.

"Come on," she told him impatiently. "There are all sorts of goodies inside. I can smell them already."

"I can't do it," Craig admitted. "There's nothing to hold on to."

"Well, there's me," decided Nosy after a moment, extending one back leg. "Hold tight, and I'll pull you up. But this should certainly prove to you that it's much better to be an ant than a Masher."

Despite the fact that she was climbing with only five legs, Nosy scampered up the paper sack with amazing ease, and when she reached the bulge at the top she shook Craig loose.

"As usual, the Masher has tried to outwit us by twisting it," she told him. "Let's hope he was careless. If he wound it too tight, I won't be able to work a passage through. Just sit here and wait for me."

Craig had to obey, and he pressed his body close to the smooth brown paper, hoping that an errant wind would not come along and blow him away. The bulge was only a slight one, and he realized that even a sneeze might throw him over the side. The worst of it was that the moment the thought came to him, he had an urge to sneeze. His nose began to itch, and he wanted to scratch it, but was afraid to take his hands from the sack to do so. They were resting, one on each side of him, palms down, and his heels were trying to dig into the paper as hard as he could make them. Soon the strain made him break out in perspiration, and that, he decided, was the best thing that could have happened, for the dampness soaked into the sack and kept him from slipping.

After what seemed a long time, Nosy returned and once again extended her back foot.

"All ready," she assured him. "I've made a little passageway, and you'll never believe the aromas that come through!"

Almost before he knew it, she had him up to the very top, and there a small spiraling hole, like the stairway in a lighthouse, wound itself downward. Craig sniffed in delight. As Nosy had said, the sack was filled with delightful odors. He recognized jelly sandwiches, and chocolate cake, ham and sweet pickles, all things he liked and had never expected to taste again.

"Hurry up," commanded Nosy. "We're entitled to fill our crops, then we must rush to the City and send out a foraging crew immediately. There's no telling how long this will be here."

Together they slid down the spiraling chute made by the twisted top of the sack, and began eating. Craig tasted a little of everything because it was all so good. Then, remembering Cricket and Jill, he filled his pockets with slivers of ham and bits of cake.

Nosy finished first, and kept urging him on to greater speed.

"We mustn't be selfish. Think of the others. We must get back and tell them about it."

Together they crept slowly up the spiraling path to the top.

"Slide down. The way you did on the mountain," encouraged Nosy.

"But that was a slope," protested Craig. "This is straight up and down. I'll fall."

"That's the idea," agreed Nosy, and pushed him over the edge.

Craig gasped, clutching at air. In the second it took him to reach the ground he was sure he would have broken bones from such a fall, but to his amazement he landed on both feet, where he stood intact. A moment later, Nosy came tumbling down beside him.

"We're alive," gasped Craig. "Nothing broke!"

"What did you expect?" Nosy demanded tartly. "Does this-tledown snap when it blows about? Come along. We must get back to the City with our news."

The scout rushed on ahead, but Craig was no longer afraid of losing her. He knew where he was, and he could find his way. He had only to follow along the petunias to the end, make a right turn and cross a small strip of grass before he reached the back flower bed beside the house. Then, if he continued straight ahead he would arrive at the back steps. In the distance he could still hear the power mower, and he was glad that Jim had always been a leisurely worker, stopping often to rest. Craig would have plenty of time to make that necessary short crossing of lawn before Jim came to it.

The dew had long since vanished, and the sun was growing warm. His parents must have arisen long ago, and he wondered wistfully what they were doing now. Were they looking for him? Perhaps they had called in the police, and his picture and Jill's were in the paper under the heading "Children Missing." He wondered what his mother and father would say if someone told them he was here under the kitchen window right now.

It took a long time to reach his destination, and more than once Craig thought resentfully of Nosy, who certainly should have been keeping a better eye on her aide than this. She hadn't once returned to make sure he was still on the right path. She had just run blithely ahead, as though she had forgotten all about him.

At last he could see the top step looming before him, and he stumbled over the hilly clods, relieved that his long walk was nearly at an end. It would be pleasant down in the cool City Under the Back Steps, and the gentle vanilla scent would be soothing after the harshly pungent smell of his mother's zinnias growing under the kitchen windows. It was funny how conscious he had become of smells. He hadn't paid much attention to them before, but now they were all around him, sweet or unpleasant, soothing or repelling. Perhaps his sense of smell was developing to match Nosy's. Craig decided he didn't care for the odor of zinnias, and he wondered why his mother had planted them.

As he drew near the entrance, he could see that something was wrong. Things were not as he had left them. Great piles of black ants were clustered about the steps, and as he approached he saw, with horror, that they were dead. Each had been as neatly decapitated as though someone had severed the head from the body with a sword. Nearby was a second pile of dead ants, but these were not black. They were red, and they were not neatly stacked, but heaped carelessly to one side, as though someone had pushed them there to get them out of the way.

As he stood staring, a line of black workers emerged from the tunnel and hurried toward their dead comrades. These they picked up tenderly, and bearing their bodies between them, they retreated and disappeared under the step.

"The undertakers!" recognized Craig. Then, turning once more to the slain red ants, "Why, there must have been a battle!"

But how could there have been? He and Nosy had spied on the Cinnamon City earlier that morning. They had seen with their own eyes the red warriors sitting quietly and being fed breakfast. But had they seen all the red army? Perhaps those idle red soldiers sitting so slothfully under the hydrangea had been left there deliberately to throw Nosy off the track. Perhaps the red ants knew they were being spied upon, and had left that group there as a trick. Probably the greater army had crept out earlier and had lain in wait to descend upon the City Under the Back Steps and once more strip its nursery.

Nursery! Jill was in the nursery! Jill must have been in the very thick of things!

Without another glance at the slain soldiers, Craig dashed into the tunnel. In the darkness, he pushed aside the toiling undertakers, dashing headlong as fast as he could down the slope to the City. The vanilla odor rushed up to meet him, but his sense of smell told him that today the vanilla fragrance was tainted with cinnamon. Perhaps, he thought, some of the intruders were still here. He fumbled in his pocket for his knife, and it felt reassuring to his touch.

There were new sentinels at the doorway, but Craig brushed off their inquiring antennae impatiently and pushed through. In the Great Hall, the black ants were already busy cleaning up the signs of the recent battle, washing and scouring the floor, carrying away the slain, seeing to the wounds of the injured.

Across the room, Cricket saw him and immediately set up an agitated noise that could not be ignored. Craig hesitated. He wanted to dash to the nursery and make sure that Jill was all right, but perhaps Cricket had important information. He decided it would be better to confer first with their friend.

Cricket lost no time imparting his news. He was full of it, and it bubbled out of him, all the while his antennae bristled with indignation.

"Jill Dear's gone. They took her away with them. I could do nothing to save her, and you weren't here with your hidden weapon, whatever it is. But I don't think they'll hurt her. They could see immediately how valuable she'd be. She had her arms full of larvae, and they just whisked her out of here, along with every egg and larva and pupa from the nursery. What are we going to do now, Cousin Craig?"

10

Like craig, jill, too, had been allowed to sleep that first night in the City Under the Back Steps, although she had trouble making Nannie see that such a thing was important.

The larvae had been carefully aired for an hour or so under the starry skies while the nursemaids stood patient, watchful guard. Then Nannie's antennae, blown by a bit of gentle wind which Jill herself considered very pleasant, had announced that the sensitive larvae might grow chilled, and that it was time they should be returned to the nursery.

Jill obediently filled her pinafore with the hairy, gourd-shaped babies, the nannies gathered up the remaining larvae in tender, careful mouths, and once more they started down the short tunnel past the cow barns and into the Great Hall.

Jill had hoped that she would be able to stop once more and speak with Cricket and Craig as she had done on her way out, but the nannies must have guessed her intention. As soon as they left the tunnel, she was snatched off her feet and rushed past the corner at such a rate of speed that she couldn't even call out. Cricket waved to her when she looked back over her shoulder, but Craig didn't even see her go by. He was fast asleep, with one of Cricket's legs laid protectively over his shoulders.

Well, she told herself, he knows that the queen is going to release us, and that's why he can sleep so calmly. She decided it was really very sensible of Craig; it made time pass more quickly. She yawned herself, realizing that she, too, was very tired. She was glad they were going back to the nursery where everyone could settle down for the night.

But she hadn't been there very long before it became clear that the nannies had no intention of settling down for a night's rest. The larvae were returned to their quarters, and immediately feeding hour began again.

"You really ought to help with this," suggested Nannie. "It serves a double purpose. We feed them, and in return the little dears give off an oil which is almost as refreshing as the milk we drink."

"I'm afraid I'm much too tired," confessed Jill. She had to keep blinking to keep her eyes open, and Nannie's voice seemed to come from a great distance. "If you'll excuse me, I think I'll just go to bed. I'm awfully sleepy."

"In the summertime!" gasped Nannie. "I never heard of such nonsense. Until Her Majesty decides to turn you out, you'll work."

"But I have to sleep for a little while," pleaded Jill. "Just till morning. Then I'll be able to work again."

"Out of the question! We'll have no sleeping sluggards here!" Nannie's antennae twitched at the idea.

"Then maybe I'd better go to the stables," suggested Jill desperately. "They like me. I'm sure they'll let me sleep for a while, and tomorrow, when I'm rested, I can carry all their cows to pasture."

Nannie shook with indignation.

"You'll do no such a thing," she retorted. "If you must sleep —if you *have* to sleep—although I consider it indolent and a waste of time—you'll do it here. You can make up for it tomorrow."

Thankfully, Jill turned and went to the room where the pupae were stored. Selecting a particularly plump one for a pillow, she nestled down next to the neat rows of silk cocoons. It would be some time before this particular group was ready to emerge, and since the pupae, at this stage, required no care, she was not likely to be disturbed by the nurses.

Her out-of-the-way sleeping place was a wise choice, and she slept undisturbed for some time. Perhaps, in the ordinary routine of the busy nurses, she was even forgotten for a time, but at last Nannie came to shake her awake. The head nurse was considerably agitated.

"Get up! Get up!" she ordered. "Fill your carrying bag with as many pupae as it will hold, and follow me."

Jill struggled to her feet. Through eyes which were still a little clogged with sleep, she saw that the nursery was filled with workers. Not all of them were regular nurses. There were engineers and garbage collectors, masseurs and grubbers, cowgirls and undertakers, and each snatched up a silken-wrapped pupa and immediately darted out the door with it.

"What is it?" gasped Jill. "What's happening?"

"War," said Nannie grimly before her mouth closed on one of the cocoons. With her antennae she motioned to Jill to carry out her previous instructions.

As rapidly as possible, Jill filled the skirt of her pinafore with pupae until it sagged with the weight. Then, obedient to the fiercely bristling antennae, she followed Nannie out of the room and into the tunnel.

Although there were no sounds from the Great Hall—in fact, Jill could never remember hearing one of the ants make any noise at all—she sensed that there was something disturbing going on in there. And even before they had rounded the last turn, she knew she had not been mistaken, for the tunnel was suddenly blocked with struggling, pushing, straining ants attempting to force their way through. For the first time she could hear sounds, an occasional click, or snap, as though a mousetrap had been sprung, but in the darkness she could not see what caused it.

Ants were pushing on every side, half of them wanting to continue on, the others bent on proceeding in the opposite direction, and her nose stung with the sharper smell of cinnamon which almost drowned out the familiar smell of vanilla. Caught in the middle as she was, Jill was afraid the pupae in her apron would be completely crushed, and she began to kick with her

feet and jab with her elbows. Neither made any dent in the hard armor of those surrounding her, but suddenly the ant in front of her fell to the ground. In her efforts not to step on the fallen worker, Jill moved and found a little space against the wall. Protecting the pupae as best she could, she managed to inch forward until she came out into the Great Hall.

Here was the wildest scene of disorder she had ever witnessed. The room was overrun with strange red ants, all of whom were dashing this way and that in uncontrollable frenzy. Although considerably smaller than the black residents of the City, they made up for their size in ferocity. Their powerful jaws, filled with sharp, formidable teeth, snapped this way and that, and every time this happened, the head of one of their black foes fell to the ground. This, Jill saw, accounted for the little clicking sounds, like closing mousetraps, which she had heard in the tunnel.

She looked around in fright, wondering where Nannie had gone, but Nannie had disappeared completely. Perhaps she was still in the tunnel, or possibly a pair of those powerful red jaws

had made an end to her. Jill fell back against the wall, wishing there were somewhere to hide. Then she heard a familiar noise. "Crick, crick, crick!" The rusty notes reverberated through the chamber, and they were the sweetest music Jill had ever heard.

Cricket was still here. Cricket was her friend. She must get to Cricket as quickly as possible.

How she ever managed to avoid those snapping steel jaws in her dash across the room, she never knew. It was always a long walk to Cricket's corner, and today it seemed to take even longer, but at last she was there, and Cricket's strong right leg was thrust protectingly around her shoulders.

"There, there," he comforted. "It will soon be over. They'll go away before long, and we'll have dinner, and I'll sing to you. Just as though it had never happened."

"Oh, Cricket," she mourned, peeping out from around his angular leg. "Why don't they defend themselves? Why don't they fight back?"

"There weren't enough soldiers, I guess," decided Cricket. "Everybody else is too busy trying to save the babies. You see, we had an unfortunate experience the last time we were invaded. The nursery was wiped out. Now all they can think about is not letting that happen again."

Undoubtedly he was right. Only the regular soldiers among the black ants were battling. The other workers were attempting to escape up the tunnel with the eggs, larvae, and pupae, but few of them were making it. Red warriors were snapping off their heads, then snatching up the babies and making off with them. From the doorway leading to the nurseries came throngs of red ants, triumphantly returning from their pillage. They carried their spoils between their legs, a single egg or pupa to a victor, which left their jaws free for battle.

"Do you think Craig's all right?" whispered Jill.

"I'm sure he is. Or at least, he's safely out of this. He left with Nosy on a scouting expedition hours ago," soothed Cricket.

"And the queen?" continued Jill. "I wouldn't want anything to happen to the queen before she has a chance to change us back."

"They won't hurt the queen. They want her to lay more eggs for next time," Cricket assured her. "But Jill Dear, about the queen——"

He broke off at the approach of two ferocious red ants who were advancing briskly toward their corner. A moment later, they halted directly in front of them, and one extended stiffly militant antennae.

"Who are you?"

Cricket drew himself up.

"I am a pet!"

"What are you good for? What do you do?"

"I make delightful music," began Cricket, but the red antennae rapped him to an abrupt halt.

"We don't need any," scorned the red warrior. "What about this one?"

"Oh, she's a pet, too," replied Cricket huffily. "She doesn't make music herself, but she enjoys hearing it."

"Stand up," ordered the second warrior, snapping her jaws at Jill. Trembling a little, she obeyed, holding her pinafore carefully before her in order not to spill the pupae.

The two red ants regarded her and the contents of her apron keenly. Their antennae conferred briefly with each other, then without another word they picked Jill up between them and began running from the Great Hall.

"Wait, wait," Cricket called after them. "You don't understand." When they did not answer, his tone grew more plaintive, and Jill could hear his words fading into the distance. "Goodbye, Jill Dear. It's been lovely knowing you."

The red ants carried her swiftly out of the tunnel and across the gray stone highway that she now knew was only the walk beside the kitchen door, then into the green jungle. Something had happened to the jungle since last night. Its tops had been cut down, so that it was no longer tall trees, but high bushes, and the trails underneath were littered with short lengths of the growth. Away off in the distance she could hear the familiar sounds of a power mower, and she knew that Jim had been cutting the back yard, and that he was now working on the other side. She wished he were close so that she could call out to him, and tell him to save her from these ruthless red savages.

The red ants ran through the cropped jungle for a long time, and Jill wondered that they didn't seem to grow tired. There were only two of them to carry her, and they were smaller than the black ants, but they must have been very strong for they showed no signs of weariness.

At last they came out in a clearing under a tall tree with wide green leaves, and Jill was dropped unceremoniously on the ground. The fall shook the breath out of her, so it was a moment before she could look around. When she recovered herself, she saw that the cleared earth all about her was littered with eggs, larvae and pupae which had been dropped there by ants who carried them, just as she herself had been dropped.

"Oh, dear," she exclaimed in unconscious imitation of Nannie. "Those poor little larvae. They'll be burned in all this heat."

But a moment later she realized that others shared the same concern. Capable black nursemaids were snatching up the larvae and hurrying away with them into a dark opening under a bushy tree. Others were gathering up eggs and pupae and carrying them underground also.

Jill sat where she was, protecting the pupae in her lap with a fold of her pinafore, staring about her. The returned warriors, without offering to help with the disposal of their spoils, were collecting in a group in the sun. She could see an occasional waving red antenna as one of them commented, perhaps on the recent battle, to her friends, but generally they seemed quite content to relax and watch the black ants work. And work they did. Even in the City Under the Back Steps, Jill had never seen such industry. Ants flew this way and that, and before long the ground was completely cleared.

It was then that Jill recognized the familiar scent of vanilla and realized that one of the black workers was hesitating at her side.

"What are you?" demanded the worker, her antennae moving across Jill's face curiously.

"I'm Jill. And I know who you are," she said eagerly. "You're from the City Under the Back Steps. I can tell by your smell."

"The egg from which I finally emerged came from there," admitted the ant. "But I've never been there myself. I live here in the Cinnamon City. I am a slave."

"A slave?" repeated Jill in horror. "But they can't do that any more. There's a law against it."

"I know of only one law. Eat without being eaten, and protect the babies. My sisters broke that law when they did not protect me. So now I am a slave. You may be very sure that I will not be a lawbreaker myself. And I see that you are not a lawbreaker, either. You have protected a whole nursery full of pupae. You must be a nannie, as I am."

"I was working in the nursery," admitted Jill, glancing down at the little white bundles in her lap. To her consternation, she saw that they were beginning to move about a little. "I think they're getting ready to come out," she told the nurse in alarm.

"Quickly!" The nurse prodded her with a commanding foot. "We must get them to the nursery. There is no time to lose. Follow me."

Jill got to her feet and, as fast as she could, followed the scurrying nursemaid to the dark hole under the hydrangea bush. The red warriors did not even glance sidewise as she passed, so confident were they that she would not try to escape.

The hole led to a dark tunnel much like the one in the City Under the Back Steps, and at the bottom was another Great Hall, much like the one with which Jill was familiar. There were, however, two great differences. This chamber was sharp with the bite of cinnamon, and in the corner there was no friendly Cricket ready to wave or to break into music.

"This way, this way," urged the nurse, rushing back. "Can't you run any faster than that?"

"No, I can't," said Jill crossly.

"Oh, I meant no offense," apologized the black nannie. "It's just that we must get them to the nursery without delay. No doubt it was exposure to sudden heat that started things a little prematurely."

When they reached the room where the other pupae had been placed, Jill saw the same confusion that she had witnessed yesterday. These pupae, like those in her pinafore, were starting to struggle from their silken cocoons, and watchful nursemaids were dashing here and there, tearing small openings in the threads to facilitate matters for the ant babies.

She carefully transferred the contents of her apron to the floor, then she, too, began to help squirming ant babies to break through their silken prisons. It took some time to accomplish all this for there were many cocoons, and Jill realized sadly that the nursery under the back steps must be completely emptied of pupae. She doubted that a single one remained, and probably not an egg or larva either, for the nurses to look after. Then she remembered those fierce snapping red jaws, and wondered if there were any nurses left in the City.

"You work well," approved one of the black nannies, coming to stand beside her. "We have never had one like you in the Cinnamon City, for our mistresses have never brought home a worker before, only babies. I can see why the black ants kept you as a slave. You are very useful."

"I wasn't a slave," protested Jill quickly. "I was a—a——"

"Were you there because you wanted to be?" demanded the nurse.

"Well, no."

"But you worked for them?"

"Yes. But you see——"

"Then you were a slave," decided the nurse. "You were a slave for them, and now you have new mistresses, and you will work for the red ants. But you must tell us what you are trained to do, for a creature such as you is new to us."

"Only what you saw," said Jill. "I helped to open cocoons and I carried things. I'm not expected to feed the babies, or anyone else."

"Very well," agreed the nurse calmly. "Since you are trained to carry things, there are undoubtedly eggs to be moved to another nursery. Come with me. I think we can promise you enough work to keep you happy and contented."

11

SLOWLY, METHODICALLY, the black ants brought the City Under the Back Steps to rights. There was a great deal to be done, and the garbage collectors had to elicit helpers from the engineers and cowgirls and nurses in order to clear the Great Hall of all traces of the recent disaster. It consumed the remaining part of the afternoon, with every ant working as hard as she could, but at last it was finished, and they all circled for a conference in the middle of the room.

There were not nearly so many residents of the City as there had been before the invasion, for the red fighters had reduced their original number by almost one half. From their corner, so far from the waving antennae that they were unable to hear what was being said, Craig and Cricket observed them curiously.

"Nosy isn't here," worried Craig. "I kept watching and watching, but she hasn't shown up. Do you think something's happened to her?"

"Possibly," agreed Cricket. Then, noticing Craig's woebegone face, he added in surprise, "Why are you so upset about Nosy? She's just another ant. There's lots of them left, and one of them will remember to feed us pretty soon."

"Nosy was different," insisted Craig. "If I could just find her, she might help me think of a plan to rescue Jill. You won't help."

"I would if I weren't so hungry," explained Cricket. "I can't be expected to think on an empty stomach, Cousin Craig, and it's been hours since I ate."

"Oh," said Craig, suddenly remembering the shreds of ham and the crumbs of chocolate cake which he had carried away from Jim's lunch sack. Cricket received them with a little chirp of delight.

"Food! You're sure it's edible?"

"Of course. It's ham and chocolate cake."

"I have never tried either," confessed Cricket, "but I shall. I am the daring member of my family. Many of us are strictly vegetarians. Others eat a little meat occasionally. But I decided, when I became a pet, that I might as well break with all tradition. After all, I have jaws for chewing. So now I eat whatever my hosts serve me."

He placed the cake crumbs on the floor before him, and began on the ham.

"Delicious," he announced after a moment. "How thoughtful of you, Cousin Craig! How kind you are to remember your old friend——" He broke off, staring at the ground where only a moment before he had placed the morsel of cake. It was no longer there.

"Those robber ants!" he cried, shaking his antennae wrathfully at the wall behind him. "The thieves! The villains! They get worse, and more daring, every day. Why, do you know, Cousin Craig, that after you left this morning, the grubbers brought in a small earthworm for breakfast and those scalawags dashed right out in the middle of the room where everyone was eating, bit off mouthfuls and got back to safety before anyone could catch them? They're multiplying, too. There's twice as many as there were yesterday."

"Didn't the ants try to plug up the hole?" asked Craig.

"Oh, yes," Cricket assured him. "There was a whole corps of engineers working on the wall, but the little villains are always breaking out in a new place." He sighed wistfully. "It looked like such good cake, too."

"Never mind," consoled Craig. "At least you had the ham. Was it enough to help you think of a way to rescue Jill?"

"I'll try," promised Cricket, and twisted his antennae around and around to aid his thought processes.

"I've got it," he declared finally. "We'll go to the Cinnamon City ourselves."

"You mean, scout it, the way Nosy and I did? Then come back and lead the black army over there?" It was the very plan which had been forming in the back of Craig's mind, but he was glad to hear it voiced by someone else.

"Not at all," objected Cricket. "The black ants never attack the Cinnamon City."

"Why not? Don't they want their babies back?"

"Oh, they'd like that well enough," admitted Cricket, "but they don't expect it. Once in a great while, an ant who has been away for a long time, returns home. But she's just been mislaid, possibly carried away in some Masher's picnic basket. She hasn't been captured. The slaves never return. The red ants wouldn't allow it. They're warriors, and these black ants of ours can't stand up to them in battle. There's no use in starting one if you know you can't win."

"But if we haven't got an army to back us up, what good will it do for us to spy on their city?" demanded Craig.

"Nor did I say anything about spying," corrected Cricket. "You were the one who said that. I said we should go there. And live. That way we will be with Jill Dear, and if an opportunity to leave presents itself, we will all depart together. Providing, of course, we don't grow fond of the place and decide to settle down permanently."

Cricket's idea didn't seem to Craig much of a plan, but he couldn't think of a better one himself. He studied the circle of ants in the middle of the hall, wondering if his friend was really right and that they would give up the loss of their babies without further struggle. At that moment, the conference came to an end, the circle broke up, and each ant resumed the regular duties which had occupied her before the invasion. They seemed quite calm, as though they were resigned to everything, and Craig sighed. Cricket must know what he was talking about.

"Do you think the red ants will let us stay in their city?" demanded Craig doubtfully.

"Of course," answered Cricket. "We're pets."

"But perhaps red ants don't want pets."

"Probably they don't," agreed Cricket cheerfully. "In that case, we'll be unwanted pets, like Spider, who used to live here with us. We'll just move in, and they'll have to feed us. Don't worry, Cousin Craig. It's done all the time."

Now that his mind was made up, Cricket saw no reason to prolong their departure. He began covering the floor of the hall in long, swooping hops, and Craig trotted along behind. When they reached the ramp, Cricket greeted each guard in turn.

"Goodbye. Goodbye. It's been so pleasant, and we've enjoyed our stay with you so tremendously that we may even return sometime."

The guards did not reply, but they moved back and allowed them to proceed up the slope and into the tunnel.

"I was afraid they wouldn't let us leave," whispered Craig.

"I don't see why you should have thought that," puzzled Cricket. "We've been guests of the City, not prisoners. You could have left any time you liked. Now with Jill Dear, it's become quite a different matter. She must work for the red rulers, since they have discovered that she is useful. That's why, when we arrive, you must convince them that you are incapable of labor in any form. You are a parasitic pet, nothing more than one more mouth to feed."

"What if they won't let us in?"

"Such a worrywart!" scolded Craig. "Don't Mashers have pets? Don't they feed them? Don't the pets sometimes appear, unasked, at the front door, and just stay on and on, and you have to give them something to eat because you can't bear to see them go hungry? Now, if you please, let's drop the discussion. I've grown quite bored with the whole thing."

Craig obediently fell silent but his thoughts were still gloomy. Even if Cricket were right and they were admitted to the Cinnamon City, even if they did manage to rescue Jill, what then? They would still be ant-size, and as such it would be dangerous to return home. Oh, if only Nosy hadn't decided to take things into her own hands just when Jill had the problem all solved. Poor Nosy! He wondered unhappily what had become of the friendly little scout.

It was night when they emerged from the tunnel. Craig looked up at the starry sky, and remembered briefly the time when such a sight had filled him with desire to explore those

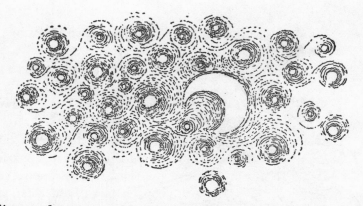

distant planets, searching for strange forms of life. How little he had realized that here on Earth, in his own back yard, was life so different from his own that he was a complete outsider. Now when he stared upward at the spangled sky he was reminded of something else. It was as though he were looking into another Great Hall, like the one below the back steps, where each star was an ant armored in sparkling silver instead of shiny black.

Then he looked away, for his nose was tingling with the rush of evening smells all around him, scents which were so different from those of the daylight hours. There was the smell of freshly cut grass, of watered flower beds, and of newly tunneled earth. The latter odor surprised him, since Jim didn't usually do any spading this late in the summer. Cricket, too, must have picked it up, for he had been vigorously waving his front legs, on which were located his organs of smell.

"Both of my noses," he announced, "tell me that night crawlers have been tunneling. Some Masher has been throwing water around, and the night crawlers have been rising up to the surface in the softened earth. They're probably all over the place."

"Oh," said Craig, marveling that such tiny excavations could account for so great a smell of fresh earth. Of course,

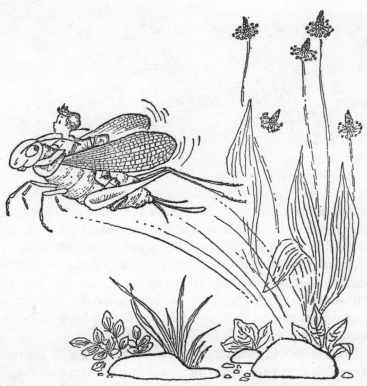

there were lots of night crawlers. He and his father had gathered them by flashlight more than once when a fishing trip was planned. These giants of earthworms always lay glistening on top of watered lawns on summer evenings but you had to be quick about picking them up or they would slide back underground.

"Would they eat us?" he asked in surprise.

"Perhaps not intentionally," admitted Cricket. "But their mouths are always open to take in food. They swallow dirt, you know, and bits of leaves and grubs, anything that clings to the soil. They have no eyes, so they just eat whatever is in their paths. And since there are so many around, I see no reason for submitting you to danger. You might step into the way of an open mouth, and not even see it in the dark. I think it best that we fly."

"But I can't fly. I don't know how."

"I do," said Cricket proudly. "Climb on my back, and keep out of the way of my wings."

The shiny black skin was slippery. It was even harder to climb than the paper sack had been, but Cricket reached around and boosted him now and then with a jab of one of his legs, and eventually Craig was settled in a little hollow where the four wings met.

"I'm all set," he panted, peering down fearfully over the side. He had the same sensation he used to have when he was on horseback; it was a long, long way to the ground.

"Better hold onto an antenna," cautioned Cricket. "We'll clip along pretty fast, once I decide which way we should go to reach the Cinnamon City."

"It's over there," Craig told him, bending one of the antennae gently to the right. "It's under the hydrangea bush. There's a fresh molehill just before you come to it, where Nosy and I spied on them."

"Very good," agreed Cricket affably, and unfurled his wings.

Clinging tightly to Cricket's antenna, Craig enjoyed the ride over the back lawn. He liked the warm, fragrant breeze in his face, the night smells all around him, and riding so high above the grass he felt more like his usual self than he did plodding along close to the roots. The trip seemed very short, compared with the long time it had taken him and Nosy to cross the same distance on foot and, almost before he knew it, Cricket had swooped down, and the closing wings jostled Craig from his slippery perch.

"Well," said Cricket brightly. "Here we are. I thought it best to settle down first and reconnoiter. As you say, it's only a jump or two from here to the Cinnamon City."

The molehill looked more than ever like a great bare mountain under the stars. Craig looked down the slope, and then drew back in alarm. Advancing toward him were three blazing torches. In the darkness, the hands which held them were invisible and the flares seemed to be suspended just a little above the ground. But they were certainly coming nearer every second.

"Cricket!" cried Craig in terror, jerking at one of the insect's back legs. "Look!"

Cricket had whirled around when he felt the jerk on his leg; now he turned and looked down the slope.

"Yes, I see," he said in mild annoyance. "Well, you can stop worrying now, Cousin Craig. Your precious Nosy is still alive."

"Nosy!"

The flares had ascended almost to the top, and now that the starlight was no longer reflected in their depth, they lost their fire. They were merely three white milky eyes, the only part of the scout's body which was visible against the dark ground.

"Nosy!" cried Craig joyfully, and rushed forward to be greeted by the trembling antennae. "What are you doing here? Did you know the City was attacked? The red ants stole Jill."

Nosy hung her head low in humiliation. Her antennae dropped, barely whispering her response.

"I know. I was fooled. I was completely taken in. I am a lawbreaker. I did not protect the babies."

"Anybody would have been fooled," insisted Craig. "It wasn't your fault at all, and I don't see how they could blame you. Why don't you go back and explain how it happened?"

"There's no excuse. No excuse," insisted Nosy weakly. "I saw it all and I could do nothing. I fought at the doorway of the City. I even did away with a few of the invaders. But there were too many of them."

"And what do you intend to do now?" demanded Cricket practically. "The others are starting all over. Why don't you?"

"Would they ever trust me again?" demanded Nosy pite-

144

ously. "Oh, I am ashamed. I will stay here, by myself, and do absolutely nothing. Idleness makes misery, and misery is the punishment of any lawbreaker."

"You mustn't do that," cried Craig. "We're going to try to save Jill. Why don't you help us, and maybe you can save some of the babies, too?"

"She wouldn't be any help," objected Cricket frankly. "You don't suppose they'd mistake Nosy for a pet, do you?"

"But perhaps they'd think she was one of their slaves," insisted Craig. "She looks just like the others. She wouldn't even need a disguise."

"Impossible." Nosy herself put an end to the discussion. "I did not protect the babies, so I am a lawbreaker. But I am not a slave. I shall stay right here and reflect upon my crime."

"She means it," Cricket assured Craig positively. "Once an ant makes up her mind about something, you can't change it. They never give up."

"Anyway, you won't starve," promised Craig. "If they let me in and out of their city, I'll bring you something to eat every day. You'll have to eat, you know."

"That is so," agreed Nosy after a moment. "If I don't eat, I should be breaking another law, and I wouldn't care to do that. Very well, I will eat what you bring me, and attempt to keep others from eating me."

"And that is all you can expect from her," declared Cricket, jabbing Craig impatiently with his front foot. "I thought you wanted to go to the Cinnamon City and see Jill Dear. Come along. Perhaps we'll be arriving at dinner time."

Craig realized that there was nothing else to do, but he hated to leave the sad little scout sitting alone on the molehill. Several times he glanced over his shoulder, hoping that Nosy would change her mind and accompany them, but the three white spots remained where they were, and finally faded entirely in the distance.

The leaves of the hydrangea bush rustled overhead as they reached it, but there were no signs of red warriors clustered about the stalks. Remembering the heap of slain black ants, Craig shivered and stayed as close to Cricket as he could. It was not difficult to do, for in the narrow tunnel Cricket couldn't spring ahead in great jumps. He had to walk, and his deliberate steps were more closely matched to Craig's than were those of the ants. At last they reached the end, and immediately two red guards, with fiercely snapping jaws, thrust bristling antennae into their faces. Cricket was in no way alarmed and addressed them jovially.

"Good evening. We are guests."

"Guests?" repeated one of the guards suspiciously. "You reek of vanilla."

"Naturally," agreed Cricket. "We just left the city of your enemies, where we were witness to your recent invasion. What havoc you wrought."

"It was a great victory," admitted the guard, but her strong right leg still barred their way into the hall below.

"We were guests there, too," confided Cricket. "Pets, you know. But after seeing the way you ants do things, we were so impressed that we decided to move over here."

"We don't want any more pets," objected the second guard. "One is plenty."

"You have a pet?" Cricket was surprised.

"A beetle. She keeps the slaves happy."

"Ah, then she is a wanted pet," said Cricket. "We are different. We are unwanted pets. You have none like us. It will take a little time before you grow to love us, but you will."

"It's true that we've never had an unwanted pet," agreed the first guard. "One never came to us before. Although I've heard that the black ants receive them. I suppose we could try it for a time. If these two don't work out, we can always chop off their heads, and let the slaves eat them for dinner."

146

"A good idea," approved the second guard, and thrust Cricket and Craig roughly ahead into the hall. "Go stay with the beetle. She'll show you around. You'll find her along one of the walls somewhere."

Cricket rustled his wings indignantly.

"Crude insects," he blustered. "What a way to treat guests. If it weren't for Jill Dear, I'd turn right around and go back."

None of the ants which crowded the Great Hall of the Cinnamon City paid the slightest attention to them as they entered. There were more black slaves in attendance than red captors whom they served by feeding and bathing and combing. This was accomplished with the same eager intensity with which those in their native city tended each other. In the center of the room was a half devoured earthworm, but only the black ants appeared to be dining from it. The red ones were leaving it completely alone.

"You'd think they'd be hungry, too," mused Cricket thoughtfully.

"Maybe they ate first," suggested Craig. "Or maybe they don't care for worms."

"Well, I do," declared Cricket. "I know that it's not good manners, Cousin Craig, but let's walk by the feast and help ourselves. I'm starving."

Although one or two of the black ants regarded them a little sharply when Cricket bent over the earthworm, none of them tried to stop him. Craig hesitated a moment but he, too, was hungry. Remembering the slug which had tasted like roast pork, he closed his eyes and allowed his own teeth to close into the white meat. He was delighted to find it slightly reminiscent of baked chicken.

"I think we'll make this our custom while we're here," confided Cricket as they started on. "We won't wait to be served. When the food is set down, we'll just help ourselves. Since the red ants haven't had an unwanted pet before, they won't think anything of it."

The guard's direction for locating the beetle had been a little vague, and Craig was afraid it might take some time. To his relief, they found her almost immediately.

She was a very small insect, no larger than the ants themselves, and was standing against one of the hard-packed clay walls, against which her yellowish brown color was almost a perfect match. At first glance, she gave the impression of being deformed, for her cylindrical head was almost as long as the rest of her body. Small tufts of hair protruded from the base of each of her antennae, and another stubby growth appeared on her back where her wings joined. Obviously, the wings were never meant for flight, since they were fused together. She stood perfectly still on her six slender legs and seemed to be observing their approach. But when they grew near, they saw that this could hardly be the case for there were no openings for eyes on her head. The mouth moved, however, in a lateral fashion and so did the six jointed antennae, which were whipping this way and that as though being blown about by a strong gale.

"Oh, the poor thing. She's blind," whispered Craig in pity.

Cricket promptly kicked him with one of his middle feet, as a sign that there were some subjects better left unmentioned, and advanced effusively toward the small yellow beetle.

"Good evening. I don't believe we've met. I am Cricket, and this is Cousin Craig. We have just arrived. Unwanted pets, you know."

The angular antennae bent this way and that, exploring Cricket's hard black coat, then moved to Craig where they lingered on his face and arms.

"I make you welcome," the beetle told them after a moment. "Although I must admit that I have never sensed anything so

148

huge as you are, Cricket. You almost frighten me. You are very strange indeed. Are you considered handsome or ugly?"

"Very handsome," snapped Cricket. "And I'm not strange at all. Cousin Craig, now, he's the one who's strange, if you're rude enough to talk about such things. I'll wager you never felt anyone like him before, now have you?"

"Why, yes, I have," objected the beetle. "There's a new slave in the nursery who feels very much as he does. She just arrived."

"Jill!" cried Craig eagerly. "She knows Jill. Is she all right, Beetle? Did they hurt her?"

"Please address me by my proper name," pleaded the blind insect. "Beetle has such a cold and impersonal sound. Call me Claviger."

Cricket snorted with disapproval and, moving away from the yellow antennae, spoke to Craig.

"Such airs!" he criticized. " 'Beetle' isn't good enough. She has to be called something else. And did you ever hear anything so rude as her remarks about me?"

"Please, is Jill all right, Claviger?" pleaded Craig again, ignoring Cricket. "You see, she's my cousin and I'm very worried about her."

"She is splendid," Claviger assured him. "The nurses are most pleased, and they'll work her day and night to keep her happy."

"Could you take us to her?" begged Craig. "I'd feel better if I saw for myself."

"Delighted to be of service," the yellow beetle told him promptly. "Just follow me."

It took Claviger a long time to arrive anywhere in the Cinnamon City, partly because she had to follow along the walls, feeling her way carefully, and partly because of the ministrations of the black ants. She seemed to be a great favorite of all of them, and one or another was always breaking off what she was doing to dash across the room and halt the beetle's progress. When this happened, Claviger stood perfectly still while the ant either fed the pet from her own crop, or licked and combed the little tufts of hair on the beetle's back.

"They certainly like you, don't they?" asked Craig respectfully.

"They adore me," agreed Claviger.

After what seemed to be an almost endless journey, the beetle led them into one of the small rooms used as a nursery where black nannies were sorting eggs. It was the first time Craig had seen inside one of the chambers in which the ants kept their babies, and he stood in the doorway staring at the great piles of eggs all arranged according to size. At that moment, an efficient nurse brushed by him, her antennae twitching sensitively.

"It's too cold in here," she warned. "There's a chill in the air. Get the carrying creature at once."

Two messengers dashed away to obey her instructions and returned, a few minutes later, pulling Jill between them.

Jill's face was red, as though she had been exercising a great deal, and she looked very tired. Before Craig could put out a hand to stop her, she had crossed the room and begun filling her apron with the white eggs.

"She's here, isn't she?" Claviger's long head wagged up and down. "I knew she'd come here if we waited long enough. They're forever moving the eggs, you know."

But Craig didn't stop to reply. He was half way across the room, already calling to his cousin.

"Jill! We're here. We've come to save you."

Jill turned and glanced over her shoulder. She looked first startled, then happy, but a moment later that expression was replaced by one of hopelessness.

"Oh, Craig! Did they get you, too?"

"Of course not. We came by ourselves, Cricket and I."

One of the black nurses touched Jill impatiently on the shoulder and the girl obediently turned and continued piling eggs into her lap.

"Aren't you glad to see us?" demanded Craig in surprise. When she didn't look up, he leaned over and also began gathering up the tiny eggs. "Here, I'll help you get through. Then we can talk."

"No!" she cried, pushing away his hand. "Don't let them know that you have pockets to carry things in. They'll never let you stop working if you do. Oh, Craig, you don't know how terrible this place is. You'd better get out of here while you still can."

12

T HIS IS REALLY the best place if you want to be in the center
of things," confided Claviger. "The small rooms are more
intimate but sooner or later everyone comes here."

She had brought Craig and Cricket back to the Great Hall,
and now they were ensconced in one corner, out of the path
of the scurrying workers and beyond biting range of any of the
scimitar-jawed red ants. Craig hadn't felt right about leaving
Jill in the nursery, not when she looked so tired and frightened,
but Cricket had convinced him that they would be safer at a
distance. They couldn't help Jill by staying there, and if they
were given a little time to think they might arrive at a plan
for effecting her escape.

"I thought you said that she could just walk out of here with
us," remembered Craig resentfully.

"I said 'if an opportunity to leave presents itself,'" corrected
Cricket. "It hasn't yet."

Craig looked around the room thoughtfully. At the moment

the red ants did not resemble mighty warriors. They plaintively opened and closed their formidable jaws, begging to be fed, and stretched their powerful forelegs lazily so that the black attendants could wash and polish them to better advantage.

"There don't seem to be any guards," observed Craig. "Except for the two at the door."

"Why should there be?" Claviger asked in surprise.

"Aren't they afraid their slaves will run away?"

"Where would they go?" puzzled the beetle, after pondering the idea for some moments. "This is their home."

"But they have another home," Craig told him. "Under the back steps."

"They wouldn't even know how to find it," declared the beetle positively. "They came here as eggs and larvae and pupae."

Craig moved back, away from Claviger's inquisitive antennae and addressed Cricket.

"Why, it's simple after all," he exclaimed. "The reason they stay here is because they don't know the way back. But you and I do. And we can lead them, and take Jill with us."

"I've got a feeling it may not be quite so easy as that," said Cricket but he spoke absently, for his eyes were on the ramp down which a group of black ants were heaving and tugging an unwieldy fungus.

"Vegetables! To go with the meat we had awhile ago," he announced joyfully. "Let's get a place at the first table."

Craig, however, was too shy to follow Cricket to the center of the hall where the grubbers finally deposited their burden. He hung back, remaining with Claviger while one after another of the black workers hurried to the feast.

"Don't the red ants like what was just brought in?" he asked the beetle. Not a single red warrior had moved from her place.

"Of course," said Claviger. "Only it has to be fed to them. Their jaws are made for biting, not chewing. If their servants didn't put food into their mouths, I don't know what would happen to them. Perhaps they'd starve."

The first ant to leave the fungus did not hurry to her red mistress. Instead, she came straight to the corner where Craig and Claviger were standing. The yellow beetle immediately opened her mouth and the ant tenderly placed a drop of liquid into the cavity. Before leaving, she gave Claviger an affectionate caress on the short bristling hairs which protruded from her back.

"They never forget," said Claviger complacently. "They always feed their pet first."

"They didn't feed me," objected Craig.

"Ah, but you are not a Claviger beetle. I am fed first, then the red ants, and you will be last."

As Craig watched, the other workers left the fungus and each scurried back to the red warrior she served. Promptly, the great sickle-like jaws swung apart, and the worker placed a drop of liquid in the dark opening.

"The red ants are quite a problem sometimes," said Claviger chattily. "They're always hungry, and they're always pestering the workers to be fed. It takes so much food to keep them going."

The fungus disappeared in a remarkably short time and Cricket waddled back. His fat little stomach hung almost to the ground, and his eyes were glazed with contentment.

"Perfectly delicious," he pronounced. "Perhaps we should consider staying here permanently, Cousin Craig. They set a far better table than the others, and no one minds how many times you come back for seconds."

Craig frowned at him, but Cricket had collapsed against the wall, entirely too full of food to care. How unfeeling of Cricket to suggest that they stay here, thought Craig. Well, he could just do as he pleased, but Craig wouldn't stay with him. He and Jill, and as many of the black workers as wanted to go, would return to the City Under the Back Steps. There was only one difficulty. Craig wasn't sure that he himself could find the way through all those intricate little trails in the grass. Everything looked so different when one was the size of an ant, and unable to see ahead more than a few inches. Once he had flown to the hydrangea bush on Cricket's back; the other time Nosy had been there to lead him—Nosy! Why, Nosy was still here! She was just outside, being miserable on top of the mole-hill. Nosy could lead them all back! The thing to do was to consult with the scout.

A black worker arrived just then with more food for Claviger, and Craig took advantage of the distraction to walk away. Cricket, who had lapsed into a contented stupor, didn't even notice.

Much to his relief, the guards let him pass with only a jab or two of their antennae.

"You're beginning to smell a little better," observed one. "More cinnamon, less vanilla. Although there's another odor that I don't recognize at all."

"Please don't forget it, though," begged Craig. "Because I'll be back and I want you to remember me."

The sun was almost up by the time Craig reached the mole-hill, and the eastern sky was a deep salmon, which made Nosy's three eyes look like pink pearls.

"Did you bring me something to eat?" asked the scout, in the martyred tone of one who is determined to do her duty. She did not seem surprised at all to see Craig so soon.

"Not yet," said Craig impatiently. "I think you're going to have to find your own food, but I've got something a lot more important to talk about."

"There is nothing more important," objected Nosy crossly. "Food is part of the law. Eat without being eaten, and protect——"

"—the babies," finished Craig. "That's what I want to talk

to you about, Nosy. If the slaves from the Cinnamon City escaped and came home, would you be glad to see them?"

"How could I be?" demanded Nosy. "I am not there. I am here."

"What I mean is," said Craig, trying hard to be patient, "if they escaped and wanted to go home, would you lead them there?"

"I can never return," Nosy reminded him sadly. "At least I wouldn't feel right about it. I failed in my duty as a scout; therefore the babies were stolen. I am to blame."

"But suppose the babies were returned. Then wouldn't everything be all right? Especially if you helped to return them?"

"Why, yes," agreed Nosy after a moment. "I suppose that would erase my crime. But I don't see how it could happen. They never have been returned once they were stolen."

"This time they're going to be. Providing you do exactly as I tell you. And providing the queen promises to change Jill and me back the way we were."

"You mean you still want to be a Masher?" asked Nosy in astonishment.

"I certainly do. And so does Jill. We don't like being ants."

"Strange. Strange," mused Nosy, shifting her position so that she regarded him out of her side eye. "What can a Masher do that an ant cannot?"

"A Masher can return those babies to your City," promised Craig boldly.

"Really?" Nosy's antennae twitched incredulously. "How?"

"I won't tell you yet. It's a secret. You know—like my secret weapon. But I can do it, providing you'll help."

This time Nosy's antennae did more than twitch. They began to flutter in excitement.

"You're sure?"

"As sure as anything."

"Then tell me what to do," begged Nosy. "Tell me at once."

"First of all," began Craig slowly, "you go to the City and talk to the queen. Tell her I've got a plan to rescue her stolen babies, but if I do she's got to promise to change Jill and me back right away."

"I will," promised Nosy. "And then?"

"Then you come back here, and I'll tell you what to do next," yawned Craig. He had suddenly grown so sleepy that he could no longer keep his eyes open. Even before Nosy had scampered to the bottom of the molehill, he was fast asleep.

The sun was overhead when he awoke to a tickling sensation on his cheek. Nosy was standing over him, her three white eyes peering down into his.

"Slothful Masher!" she reproved impatiently. "Letting the warm sunshine go to waste while you sleep. Get up. Get up, and fetch the babies."

"Did you see the queen?" demanded Craig, wide awake at the instant. "What did she say?"

"She was incredulous at first, naturally. Just as I was," explained Nosy. "She didn't believe that such a thing could ever be brought about. But after a time I was able to convince Her Majesty that it was possible you Mashers may have stumbled onto some secret which is as yet unknown to us ants. I reminded her of your secret weapon——"

"But what did she say?" broke in Craig. "Did she promise to change us back?"

"Yes," said Nosy, but her antennae jerked with irritation at the interruption. "Her Majesty is most gracious. If you and I are able to rescue the babies, she will not only pardon me for my great crime, but she will change you back into a Masher."

"Good!" Craig jumped to his feet. "Now, I'll tell you what to do next, Nosy. You stay right here, while I go back in the Cinnamon City and bring out all the workers."

"Why should you bring the workers? It's the innocent babies we must save."

"If we bring the workers, they'll bring the babies," explained Craig. "They couldn't leave them behind, or they'd be breaking the law. Besides, the workers used to be babies themselves. They were stolen, too. Wouldn't they be welcome in your City?"

"Very welcome," agreed Nosy heartily. "They are our sisters."

"Well, they want their freedom," said Craig. "They want to come home, but they don't know the way. It will be your job to lead them back to the City. Can you do that?"

Nosy drew herself up proudly.

"I am a scout," she reminded him. "There is no trail which I cannot unravel."

Craig nodded, and turned to descend the molehill, but he stopped upon seeing that Nosy was preparing to accompany him.

"You can't go," he objected. "You have to stay here, where I can find you again when I come back with the others."

"I shall be back by that time," Nosy assured him. "But now that I am almost cleared of being a criminal, I must take care to break no more laws. It is time that I ate, and since the Cinnamon City pastures its cows upon that rosebush yonder, I must go and fill my stomach and crop."

"Won't they recognize you for a stranger?" worried Craig.

"I shall keep my distance from the herders," promised Nosy. "And the cows won't care."

As soon as he re-entered the Great Hall of the Cinnamon City, Craig hurried to rejoin Cricket and Claviger. The yellow beetle received him calmly, but Cricket, by this time thoroughly awake, was considerably disturbed.

"I declare, Cousin Craig, it was naughty of you to worry me this way. You might have left word that you intended to take a walk. Poor Claviger couldn't see which way you went and the ants were far too busy to notice."

"I'm sorry, Cricket," apologized Craig. "But I have the best news. I've been outside, talking to Nosy. And she's been to see the queen, the black ant queen. She's promised to change Jill and me back to our regular size. All we have to do is lead all the workers here to the City Under the Back Steps."

"Oh, no," cried Claviger in alarm. "You can't! You mustn't! Why, what would become of me if you took all my friends away?"

"We'll take you, too," promised Craig quickly. "You'll like living there lots better than here. There'll be twice as many black ants to make a fuss over you. And no red ones at all."

"Twice as many!" Claviger's little jaws snapped with delight. "And no red ones! Oh, that will be pleasant. To tell you the truth, I don't care for the red soldiers, and I don't think they're too fond of me. Would you believe it, they seem to resent it when my friends feed me before they do them?"

"You can hardly blame them for that," objected Cricket.

"But I do," pouted Claviger. "If one has a pet, one must take care of it. Why, if I'm hungry, the ants even feed me before they feed their own babies. That's why I'll be glad to move to a city where everyone is my friend."

"Since she feels that way," said Cricket thoughtfully, "it might be a good idea to have her approach the black ants and tell them what you have in mind. I'd do it myself, but none of them has shown the slightest indication of wanting to speak to me."

It was a little difficult making the yellow beetle understand exactly what they wanted her to do, but once she did, she was agreeable. She was to contact every black ant in the Cinnamon City with the information that freedom was at hand. The former captives were to gather on the molehill outside, where an experienced scout would be waiting to lead them to their native city. They were advised to leave in small groups, so as not to alert the red warriors, and the nannies were to bring Jill, as well as all the babies in the nursery.

"And someone must bring me," interrupted Claviger at this point.

"I'll bring you myself," promised Cricket. "You may ride on my back, and we'll fly there before anyone."

It was decided that Craig and Cricket should start out right away and await the arrival of the others on the molehill. They had no part in imparting the news of the escape, and once the black ants began their exodus, the tunnel would be quite full enough.

They came out into the blazing heat of midafternoon, and after the coolness of the underground it made Craig feel a little dizzy. Cricket lingered a moment in the shade of the hydrangea bush, muttering resentfully that it would have been better planning to set out in the evening. Nosy, however, who awaited them atop the molehill, did not mind the heat at all. Instead it inspired her to activity, and since she had promised not to leave her station, she was running around and around the top of the mound in happy little circles that led nowhere at all.

"Are they coming? Where are they?" She halted to greet them, her antennae playing anxiously from one to another.

"They'll be here," promised Craig. "They have to sneak out without being seen, you know."

Cricket collapsed on the shady side of the hill, and began covering himself with dirt.

"Wake me when it's cool," he panted. "If you want to leave before then, just go on without me. I can't stir until that miserable sun goes down."

Craig sat down to wait, his eyes on the entrance to the Cinnamon City, but Nosy was far too excited. She resumed her circling of the molehill, pausing every once in a while to ask how long it would be before her sisters arrived with the babies. Craig couldn't answer. He could only beg her to be patient.

Claviger was slow. It would take some time before she made the rounds of the city.

But as the shadows grew longer, even Craig began to feel that the ants were being a little too deliberate about breaking away. Several times he thought the first group was coming toward the molehill, but it always turned out that the workers he saw were bent on some other undertaking. Grubbers left and returned with food. A group of nannies came from the entrance, then climbed the old rosebush which grew next to the hydrangea for a supply of fresh milk. New cowgirls replaced those who were on duty, and those who were relieved scurried back into the City. Not even a single ant approached the molehill.

"I knew it wouldn't work," reproached Nosy. "It was cruel of you to make me believe that I could ever be forgiven for my crime."

"It's that yellow beetle," scowled Craig. "That Claviger! We should never have trusted her to spread the news. We should have done it ourselves."

They were still waiting when the sun went down. On the lawn behind them, a mother robin began teaching her speckled breasted brood to hunt worms, and now Craig felt that he had to divide his attention between the doorway to the Cinnamon City and the birds. They were terrifyingly large, and their yellow beaks looked like great golden swords. They tilted their heads to hear the tunneling of worms in the ground, and Craig was almost afraid to breathe for fear they would hear him, too, even from this distance.

Cricket woke up, shook off the earth with which he had covered himself, and waddled around to join them.

"I see that no one's arrived yet, so I haven't missed anything," he said. "Would you care for a little music to pass the time while we're waiting?"

"No, thanks," said Craig, with a quick glance toward the robins.

"It was too much to expect," mourned Nosy. "No one's coming."

"Oh, yes, they are," said Cricket mildly. "Someone just came out the doorway. It's Claviger. She must have brought a reply to the message."

The yellow beetle had, indeed, emerged from the hole under the hydrangea, and now she stood, her eyeless head turning this way and that, her jointed antennae bending and straightening inquiringly.

"I'd better get her," decided Cricket. "She'll never find her way over here."

There was a whirring sound as he took off from the molehill, and in a second or two they saw him alight under the bush. He and Claviger conferred briefly, and the yellow beetle managed to scramble onto the shiny back of the larger insect. Then they were in the air.

Craig almost forgot the danger of the robins in his excitement at seeing Claviger. As soon as Cricket settled down he began his questions.

"What happened? Didn't you tell them? Did the red ants suspect something, and keep them from escaping? How come you're all by yourself? Did they send a message by you?"

"I don't think they sent a message," said Claviger thoughtfully, answering the last question first. "At any rate, they didn't ask me to relay it to you."

"But didn't you talk to them? Didn't you have a chance to explain about the escape?"

"Oh, yes," nodded Claviger. "I talked with them. I talked with the engineers and the nurses, the cowgirls and the doctors, the undertakers and the grubbers and masseurs. I talked with all of them, and explained the whole thing quite carefully. But they all had the same answer, so I ended up by coming by myself. I seem to be the only one who could, you see."

"But what was it they all said?" insisted Craig. "After you told them about the escape, what did they say?"

"They said they had work to do," Claviger told him. "They said they were much too busy to take the time to escape."

13

"IT SEEMS TO ME," said Cricket, "that there's only one thing to do. Think of another plan. And since the last plan was mine, it's your turn to think of it, Cousin Craig."

"The last plan was not yours," objected Craig. "I thought of leading the black ants back home. You didn't."

"Ah, but that plan didn't work," Cricket reminded him. "My plan, about coming to live in the Cinnamon City, was successful. We were able to do it, so it was a good plan. Your plan didn't work at all, so you'll just have to think of another."

Craig sighed. At least part of what Cricket said was true. They had been over and over the matter with Claviger, and the yellow beetle was very firm in maintaining that the black slaves would not attempt an escape so long as there was work to be done.

"But they could work just as well at home," fumed Craig.

"Of course they could," agreed Cricket calmly. "The problem is to get them there."

Nosy took no part in the discussion whatever. She had slumped down on the molehill, her antennae drooping hopelessly over each of her side eyes, as she gave herself up to a life of useless misery.

"I sense a strange noise," said Claviger suddenly. "The outside world is filled with strange noises, but this one has just begun. It's a watery 'whoosh, whoosh.'"

Craig, too, had heard this new sound, and now he glanced toward the house which loomed large in the twilight far, far away across the lawn.

"It's Jim," he recognized. "Our handy man. Mother's got him to come back after supper and spray the roses for her."

"What does that mean?" wondered Cricket.

"Oh, there's some kind of poison in the spray," explained Craig carelessly. "It's to kill the little green bugs that eat the roses."

"Bugs!" cried Cricket in horror. "Bugs indeed! Those are the cows which belong to the ants. So it's the Mashers who are to blame when whole herds are wiped out overnight."

"What's this? What's this?" exclaimed Claviger. "I've never heard of anything so terrible."

"Don't tell me that the red ants have never lost their herds," said Cricket sharply. "It happens several times every summer to the City Under the Back Steps. That's why breeding stock is always kept safely in the underground stables."

"No," decided Claviger after a moment. "I don't think it ever has. At least, I've never heard of it."

"Mother doesn't care much about the old rosebush down here," remembered Craig a little uncomfortably. "Her best ones are up by the house. She's always saying she's going to have this old buggy one taken out one of these days."

Remembering his mother, he felt miserable and lonesome once more. He wondered what she was doing up there in the house, and wished he dared creep inside and try again to make her notice him.

"Losing our best herd is one of our greatest disasters," mourned Cricket. "The grubbers have to work twice as hard bringing home food when that happens. In fact, almost everyone turns into a grubber then—the nurses, the cowgirls, the engineers, everyone. They all have to concentrate on filling the larder in order not to break the law."

The sounds of the distant spray gun stopped, and Craig tried once more to concentrate on his immediate problem. Surely there must be some way to convince the black ants that they should take time away from their duties to escape. Once they were safely home, they could resume work as hard as ever before.

"Look sharp!" warned Cricket suddenly, his front leg closing around Craig's waist. "We may have to jump. The Masher's coming this way."

"Don't leave me! Don't leave me!" cried Claviger in alarm. "I'm only here because of you, remember."

Sure enough. Jim was coming across the lawn, and he was carrying something made of metal. Craig could hear its clink against the buttons of his jacket. But he turned off before he came to the molehill, and went straight to the old rosebush next to the hydrangea. A moment later the "whoosh, whoosh" of the spray gun started anew.

"I guess he's decided to spray the old rosebush this time," whispered Craig. "Maybe Mother changed her mind about digging it up."

"Dreadful, dreadful," cried Claviger.

"It seems only fair that the red ants suffer the same disaster as the black ants," said Cricket virtuously. "Although it will work a hardship on the poor slaves. Without their milk supply, they'll really have to hustle to find food for themselves and their savage mistresses, too."

"Oh, dear. Oh, dear," moaned Claviger. "My poor babies! And I had thought I had found them such a good home!"

"What have your babies got to do with all this?" puzzled Cricket.

"Why, it's very simple," Claviger told him. "Last summer I laid my eggs close by, underground, you know, where they'd be safe. They hatched into grubs, and I don't mind admitting that was a scary time. If the ants had found them, they'd have gobbled them up at once. I shivered every time a grub was brought inside the Cinnamon City, but I'm thankful to say that I was too clever for the ants. They didn't find one of mine. Any day now, my children will emerge as lovely full grown Claviger beetles like their mother, and I had hoped that we could all live together in the Cinnamon City. It was such a beautiful plan."

"It won't work now, though," insisted Cricket. "The red ants wouldn't let you take them inside when there's a food shortage. And even if they did, your children would starve before the black ants got around to feeding them."

"No such a thing," Claviger objected indignantly. "The red ants wouldn't stop my children from entering, for the black ants would carry them in. And we would be fed first, so we wouldn't starve."

"Somebody'd starve," began Cricket, but Craig interrupted him.

"Cricket! Do you suppose that would work? Ants have to eat, or they break their law. If we took most of the food away from the Cinnamon City, wouldn't the black ants be willing to go home where there was plenty of it?"

"They might. But I don't see how we could do that," argued Cricket.

"About the only way is to eat it up as fast as it comes in," said Craig. "Their cows are gone now, so they haven't any milk. They'll have to depend on what the grubbers can find. Claviger's telling the truth about them feeding her first. I saw them do it myself. Claviger, how many babies do you have?"

"Oh, many," remembered Claviger fondly. "Six, ten, twelve. How can I be sure? Grubs are always being eaten."

"When will they be hatched?"

"Today, tomorrow, next week," mumbled Claviger vaguely. "Perhaps they're here this minute. Those things are always uncertain."

"*You* can always eat a lot," declared Craig, patting Cricket approvingly. "And I can hold my share, but we still ought to have somebody who can snatch it away the minute the grubbers bring it in."

"Hm," sniffed Cricket. "It's too bad they don't have a nest of robber ants, if that's what you want."

"Robber ants!" cried Craig in delight. "Nosy, will you—" But one glance at the dejected little scout convinced him that he could expect no help from that quarter.

"Cricket, we'll have to go back to the City Under the Back Steps," he declared. "Somehow, we've got to convince those robber ants to move over here."

"I'll go with you," offered Claviger. "If there's going to be a food shortage in the Cinnamon City, I might as well leave, too."

"And leave your babies?" demanded Craig, scandalized.

"They can take care of themselves, the little darlings," boasted Claviger proudly.

"You'll have to stay and wait for them," insisted Craig. "It's your duty. You must show them what to do. They may be bashful about saying that they're hungry."

"Not my children," maintained Claviger stoutly.

In the end, Cricket carried the yellow beetle back to the base of the hydrangea bush, close to the spot where she was certain she had buried her eggs last summer. Then he returned to the molehill, and it was Craig's turn to scramble up to the little dent where the wings tucked in, and they were off, leaving Nosy alone with her sorrow.

The warm vanilla scent which rushed up to meet them as they walked under the bottom board filled Craig with a curious feeling of happiness. He was back—back in the City ruled by the black ant queen who had the power to restore him and Jill to their normal sizes. Moreover, he was working on a plan which might bring this thing about. Hadn't the queen given her promise? He refused to consider the possibility that this plan, like the first one, might fail. It couldn't fail! He wouldn't let it!

As they came out onto the ramp, he could see that a conference of some kind was in progress in the Great Hall, for the ants were ringed in a circle.

"What's going on?" asked Cricket curiously, standing still while he gave the sentinel at the door an opportunity to recognize him.

"Trouble," the guard told him. "Our best herds were wiped out this evening." She turned her antennae to Craig, touching him delicately. "I recognize you both, in spite of the distasteful tang of cinnamon that clings to you. But you couldn't have returned at a worse time. We're all going on short rations immediately."

"Our stay may be brief," admitted Cricket.

As they started across the hall toward the corner, Craig had a terrifying thought.

"Cricket!" he cried in a worried tone. "What if we do bring all those black ants back here, and the guards don't recognize them? After all, most of them left as eggs and larvae. There isn't too much vanilla smell about them any more."

"There's enough," scoffed Cricket. "Any ant can recognize the egg from her own city, or the ant which came from that egg. She never loses all the scent, no matter how long she's been away. Don't waste time worrying about such things.

169

You'd better worry instead about how you're going to induce the robber ants to move."

The wall in which the robber ants made their home looked as though it had chicken pox. The ants themselves were so small that they required only tiny openings to the intricate maze of tunnels within the hard packed earth, but each one showed. Many of them had been stopped up by the City engineers, but the robber ants were tireless workers and not easily discouraged. As fast as one hole was closed, they opened two more, for they, like their larger cousins, obeyed the law which bade them eat.

Since there was no food in sight at the moment, it was not strange that the robber ants, too, were invisible. But Craig was sure they were close at hand. They never knew when something to eat would be brought into the City, and when that happened, they must be prepared to dart out and snatch their share. He wished now that he had brought something to tempt them from their hiding places, but such a thing had not occurred to him before. He wanted to call out to them, but he knew it was useless to do so. They could not hear his voice; he had to reach them through their sense of touch. But how could he possibly touch one of them through that great barrier of earth?

"Well?" asked Cricket expectantly.

Craig took a deep breath and stepped over to the wall. Just in front of him was a freshly opened hole. He covered it with the palm of his hand and stood there waiting. For a minute nothing happened. Then his palm was touched lightly, as though by the tip of a feather, and he heard the robber ant.

"What is this strange thing? What are they using now, instead of earth, to block our entrance ways?"

"I am a friend," cried Craig. "I'm not blocking your entrance way. I want to talk—to communicate."

The featherlike touch on his hand fluttered for an instant, then as though curiosity had lent bravery, it grew firm.

"Friend? We have no friends."

"Oh, yes you have. You have two friends. Cricket and me."

"Oh, Cricket. We know him," admitted the robber ant. "He never did us harm, but he never did us good, either. You, we do not know at all."

"Just the same, I'm your friend," insisted Craig. "And so is Cricket. And we want to prove it to you."

"How?"

"Did you know that the City just lost all its cows? They were poisoned. Food's going to be pretty short around here for a while."

The antennae jabbed against his hand with surprise, then, for a few moments disappeared entirely. Obviously the robber ant was conveying this startling news to her friends. Craig stood perfectly still and waited. He was pretty certain that she would return for more details. After a time she did.

"Thank you," said the robber ant. "You have saved us some hungry days by giving us this information early. You are a friend."

"What do you plan to do now?" demanded Craig quickly.

"Why, move, of course. To another city. Our scouts must leave at once to find one which will be suited to our needs."

"I know of one," Craig told her eagerly. "It's a red ant city, but there are lots of black ants who bring in plenty of food. And we could take you there tonight, Cricket and I. You wouldn't have to walk, either. You could fly. Cricket would carry you and save you lots of time."

"Such a decision concerns the whole community," admitted the robber ant. "You must give us a chance to confer."

This time she was absent for some little while. Craig took his hand from the opening to rest his arm, which was beginning to grow very tired from being held so long in such a position. He relayed his conversation with the robber ant to Cricket, who objected strenuously on hearing that he was expected to convey the small insects to the Cinnamon City.

"And another thing, I'm no friend to creatures who used to snatch food from my mouth," he protested. "You should never have told them that I was."

"Maybe you weren't their friend then," argued Craig, "but you will be now. Especially if you carry them there. They'll be under obligation to you, and if you're under obligation to somebody you certainly couldn't steal his food."

"You couldn't?" Cricket was skeptical, but hopeful.

"Of course not."

"Very well," decided Cricket. "I'll carry them. Only they must promise not to squirm around and tickle."

After a further lengthy delay, two tiny antennae protruded from the hole in the wall, to be followed by the small head to which they were attached. It was as far as the robber ant was willing to advance into the room. Craig walked over and extended one finger.

"It has been decided that we will accept your kind offer to fly." The antennae caressed his finger, while the small frontal eyes regarded him shyly. "But we feel that it would be better for everyone concerned to meet you above ground. We should hate to disturb out present hosts at their meeting."

"It's a good idea," agreed Craig, looking over his shoulder. The council, which had been called to discuss the loss of the cows, was still in progress. When he looked back, the robber ant had disappeared from the opening.

The sentinel at the door saw them coming, and deliberately turned away. Perhaps she was glad that they had decided not to remain longer. Two more mouths to feed in a time of crisis might be something of a problem.

"How many trips do you think it will take to get all the

robber ants to the hydrangea bush?" asked Craig, as once more they toiled up the tunnel.

"It depends on how many there are," said Cricket practically. "They live in smaller colonies than the other ants, though, and I hope we can do it all at once. It seems to me that lately I spend all my time flying. It's been ages since I've made any music."

Although the robber ants themselves modestly insisted that theirs was but a small colony, it seemed to Craig, when he stepped out into the starlight and saw the great swarm of tiny insects grouped about the entrance, that there were a great many of them. He was glad of their numbers. The more there were, the more food they could snatch away from the residents of the Cinnamon City.

They were shy little ants, and outside of one of their number, possibly the ant with whom he had spoken before, they darted away whenever he moved in their direction. They stared at him curiously out of their many eyes, and their little antennae waved toward him, as though groping to pick up a scent, but they would not permit him to come within speaking range.

Cricket was another matter. They had seen his kind before. They had, as he said, snatched away his very dinner before he could eat it. They considered him harmless, and the moment he appeared they began crowding so thickly on his back that he could not unfurl his wings.

"Get down," scolded Cricket. "Stop crowding. If you expect me to fly, you'll have to give me room."

They finally understood, and those who had settled over his wings unloosened their grasp, clutching instead one of the legs of a sister who had availed herself of a more satisfactory position. Cricket's back was completely covered with robber ants; they even clung to his legs, and would have hung onto his antennae as well had he not pushed them off. When he finally managed to open his four wings, some of those still on the

173

ground grasped a leg of one of their sisters who had found herself a seat, so that as Cricket rose off the earth, he seemed to be trailing little streamers of ants after him.

"It's too many for the first load," protested Craig to the robber ant who had been delegated as his contact. "Cricket can hardly clear the ground when he has to carry so many."

"They're so excited," explained the robber ant. "You can't blame them for not wanting to wait any longer. You see, only

the queens can fly. Those workers never expected to, poor dears, although it's always been their fondest dream. I think the promise of flying there was what decided the council to accept your offer to lead us to a new city."

It took three trips for Cricket to transport all the robber ants to the hydrangea bush. The last load was small, and included Craig and the spokesman. Most of the others had been far too impatient to delay their one and only flight into the air a moment longer than was necessary.

By this time Cricket was very tired. He settled down under the hydrangea with a heavy thud that sent robber ants scattering in every direction.

"That does it," he groaned. "I'm going to have to rest for six weeks to make up for this one evening."

Craig patted the hard black head sympathetically before sliding down the slippery sides. The robber ant was politely awaiting him on the ground.

"If we don't meet again, thank you for arranging this pleasure," she said graciously.

"You're welcome," said Craig automatically, but his eyes were searching the spaded ground around the bush. He had expected it to be crowded with tiny ants, but except for himself, Cricket, and the spokesman there was no one to be seen. "Your friends?" he asked. "Where did they go?"

"Underground," explained the robber, with a farewell wave of her antennae. "We've a lot of tunneling ahead of us, and we wouldn't want to miss breakfast."

A moment later, she, too, had disappeared, and so swiftly that Craig couldn't be quite sure where she had gone.

"Well," he said, turning to Cricket. "So far, so good. Jim did away with their cows. You and I brought the robber ants. Now we'll find Claviger, and——"

He broke off as something hard and prickly jabbed against his neck.

175

"I sense that you are my friend," said a voice in his ear. "I have been looking for a friend, someone to escort us to the doorway of the Cinnamon City."

Craig whirled around. Behind him stood Claviger, her jointed antennae bent in sharp angles of pride. A new moon was just sliding over the edge of the Johnsons' house next door, and together with the stars shed its light on her and what seemed to be a long line of her replicas which trailed behind to disappear into the grass. Claviger had been lucky. Fifteen of her babies had hatched safely.

14

UNDOUBTEDLY THE TRAGEDY to their dairy herd was reported immediately to the Cinnamon City, but Craig and Cricket decided that since it was the first time the red ants had suffered such misfortune they must not have realized the enormity of their loss. Otherwise, when a black worker finally emerged from under the hydrangea bush and laid tentative antennae on the sizable crowd of Claviger beetles clustered about, she would not have greeted them with such an obvious display of enthusiasm. She scurried from one to another, caressing them each in turn, then with a last appreciative lick, turned and disappeared into the hole.

"Did she tell you to go away?" Craig asked Mother Claviger. He and Cricket, both of whom had been ignored by the ant, couldn't help feeling a little left out of things.

"Not at all," denied Claviger in surprise. "She said to wait right here. She doesn't want us to get tired out by the long walk. She's gone to get friends to carry us down the tunnel."

"They haven't even thought about the extra food it will take to feed all these beetles," whispered Craig. "But when they remember, and when the robber ants really get going——"

"Don't even speak of them," shuddered Cricket. "They may be under obligation to me, but I'd much rather call the whole thing quits and forget them as soon as possible."

Before long the worker returned with her promised friends, all of whom seemed quite as excited as she had been to see the large family of yellow beetles. They picked up Mother Claviger and her children tenderly, and soon disappeared into the dark hole under the hydrangea.

"I suppose we might as well go, too," said Cricket a little huffily.

"Yes," agreed Craig. "Because if the grubbers bring in any food, I want you to eat as much as you can."

"Oh, you can trust me," promised Cricket, with a slight return of his former good spirits.

Because Cricket was so tired from all his flying, they walked slowly, and as a consequence arrived in the cinnamon-scented city considerably behind the workers and the Claviger family. They had half suspected to find that the entrance would be barred by the red guards, who certainly should not have welcomed the addition of so many hungry pets, but instead they found the sentinels in a mood which almost approached friendliness. Below, in the Great Hall, they could see that the Clavigers were now encircled by a throng of adoring black workers, each of whom clamored for her turn to caress the fat little beetles.

"So you're back," observed the guard, poking Craig and Cricket in turn. "And did you, too, bring us a new milk supply?"

"What do you mean, 'too'?" asked Cricket cautiously.

"It's very simple," answered the guard. "Something happened to our cows which are kept pastured in the outer world.

The slaves were quite upset about it for a time, but they've found a new source of milk, so there's nothing to worry about any more. One of them just brought me a serving, and I must admit that it's sweeter and more delicious than the kind we used to have."

"I don't understand," began Craig, but Cricket kicked him warningly.

"Congratulations," Cricket applauded, punctuating his remark with a small "crick" from his wings. "You ants certainly do things well in your city."

"What did she mean by a new source of milk?" demanded Craig as soon as they had passed down the ramp and into the hall. "Did they find another herd of cows somewhere?"

"I haven't the slightest idea," admitted Cricket. "As soon as that mob thins out around the beetles, we'll ask Claviger. Maybe she's heard something."

But it was some time before the Claviger family was without attendant ants. Workers were constantly coming and going. A group of grubbers arrived, tugging and pushing a soft grayish grub. Upon seeing the sixteen beetles, they immediately dropped their burden and hurried over to pay their respects.

With a happy click of his jaws, Cricket began waddling toward the forgotten tidbit, but even before he had reached it, a half dozen tiny ants had darted out of one of the walls, snapped off a morsel, and were on their way back to their hiding place. Cricket drew back in distaste, and such residents of the Cinnamon City who chanced to observe this pillage, flourished their antennae in indignant surprise, but Craig jumped up and down and cheered. His plan was working out! The robber ants were on the job!

After a moment Cricket recovered himself and continued toward the grub, where he began to dine. He was joined immediately by several black workers, who were also determined to get their share, but most of the ants had not even noticed the in-

179

cident. However, the news that robber ants had moved in finally got around. Perhaps, when the grubbers had finished paying their respects to the beetles, they asked about their recent contribution to the public larder. It had been a small grub, and by that time had completely disappeared. Craig observed that the ants who had shared the grub first fed the beetles and some of their red mistresses, then began scurrying from one to another of their black sisters. They conferred briefly, then separated, and each went on to another ant, relaying the information.

After a few minutes, a group of engineers proceeded to the wall which housed the robber ant colony, and began patching up the holes. Since the Clavigers were at last alone, Craig joined them to ask if they knew anything about the new milk supply. He went by himself, for Cricket, who had managed to consume most of the grub, was entirely too full to walk.

"Why, certainly," said Mother Claviger a little complacently. "Although milk is hardly the proper name for it. The sweet syrup that my children and I make is more like candy. The ants never grow tired of it, and it's so nourishing, too."

"But I didn't know," cried Craig. "You never said anything about you giving them milk."

"I didn't like to brag," explained Claviger. "Besides, since you have eyes I presumed that you could see for yourself. When stroked, the little hairs on my back give off delicious syrup.

That's why I knew the ants would welcome all my family, even with a food shortage. We feed them—they feed us. It's fair enough, don't you think?"

"I suppose so," agreed Craig reluctantly. "Only what if there's not enough food for them to feed you?"

"I worried about that at first, but it's all been worked out," said Claviger happily. "My children and I are going to the nursery. From now on, we'll be expected to give our delicious syrup only to those who take care of the babies. That won't be such a demand on us, you see. For the time being, everyone but the nannies is going to have to be a grubber."

Craig glared at Mother Claviger and the children who were so like her that it was almost impossible to tell one from another. Sixteen eyeless heads were all tilted in his direction, and thirty-two antennae bent in angular curiosity, as though waiting to hear what he would do next. Well, there wasn't much he could do now. They were here, and unless the food shortage grew so acute that it was felt in the nursery, there was no way he could get them to leave again. The nursery, of course, would be the last part of the City to suffer privation.

He turned and started to walk away, but Mother Claviger must have sensed his anger, for she reached out and touched him graciously.

"I've so enjoyed our acquaintance," she assured him. "If we don't meet in the nursery, perhaps we will some evening when they bring us outside for our airing with the larvae."

Cricket, who still suffered from his recent feast, only managed to wave a shocked antenna when Craig reported what had happened.

"I've known lots of beetles, big ones and little ones, but I've never known a Claviger before," he confessed. "They're rare about these parts. Immigrants, probably. The beetles I've known certainly don't give milk."

"But what can we do about it?" demanded Craig.

"Nothing," Cricket decided. "Much as I dislike them, I think we're going to have to depend on the robber ants. Their colony will grow pretty fast. They sent out an alarm, and brought all their distant cousins when they came here. And maybe you didn't notice, but they carried along any number of eggs and larvae and pupae."

The robber ants were, indeed, a dependable ally. Although the Cinnamon City was now on the alert, neither the black workers nor the red soldiers, who had decided that this was warfare worthy of their efforts, proved fleet enough to capture one of the swift little marauders before she reached safety. The engineers worked tirelessly repairing the wall, but like those in the City Under the Back Steps, they were unable to keep up with the new openings.

From time to time groups of grubbers brought food into the hall, and each time the unwelcome residents of the wall got away with some of it. Cricket, too, managed to swallow some of each delivery, but Craig saw that his eyes were beginning to glaze, and his stomach now dragged on the ground.

Before long, the red warriors gave up their part of the chase. It became clear to them that it was impossible to snap up one of the robbers in their powerful jaws, and now they were more concerned with the delay in their own next meal. They were always hungry, and when not engaged in active warfare, they spent most of their time teasing their black servants to share the sweet liquid stored in their crops. But now the crops were empty, and there was not enough food on hand to refill them. The Clavigers had long since been escorted to the nursery, and although parties of grubbers brought in occasional offerings of meat or vegetables or grain, there was barely enough for the first stomachs of the black workers, certainly not enough left over to share.

"You know," said Cricket uneasily, "this could turn into a very bad situation. I think we should leave here."

"But why?" demanded Craig. "Everything's going just as we planned. It couldn't be working out better."

"True," agreed Cricket. "So it would have to work out worse. And it could, especially for us. I don't like the way that red ant over here has been eying us. I don't at all. She has a hungry look."

"Of course she has," chuckled Craig. "And she'll get even hungrier."

"Hungry enough to enjoy crickets? And Mashers? Oh, she couldn't chew us up herself. But she could snap off our heads. And once we were dead, we might as well be eaten. Waste not, want not, you know."

It was Craig's turn to observe the red warriors uneasily. A small group of them stood only a little distance away. Their ponderous jaws opened and closed pleadingly whenever a black ant moved toward them, but it seemed to him that those many side eyes were observing him and Cricket with speculation.

"Maybe you're right," he agreed hastily. "I think we can leave everything to the robber ants. Maybe we ought to go see how Nosy's getting along."

When they came out of the tunnel, a group of toiling grubbers had just hauled an orange and brown caterpillar to the entrance. They had stopped momentarily to confer on the best way to maneuver the insect down the slope, and Cricket took advantage of the pause to address one of them.

"A fine catch!"

"It took us a long while to bring it in," admitted the grubber. "We had to hunt farther afield than we usually do to find this one."

"Ah, game is growing scarce around here?"

"Yes, and it takes so much more now," explained the grubber as she resumed her place in line.

"The first thing we know, the grubbing parties from the Cin-

183

namon City will be poaching on the territory around the back steps," Cricket told Craig thoughtfully.

"Aren't they allowed to? Is it against the law?"

"Oh, there's no law against it. You take food where you find it, of course. But it's not usual to go so far. Would you walk 3000 miles for one pot roast in a single day?"

"Of course not," denied Craig scornfully. "Nobody can walk that far."

"Ants do. It's a matter of comparative size, remember. From the hydrangea bush to the back steps would be roughly 2000 miles, and they'd easily make up the other thousand in their normal running around."

"Nosy used to make that trip twice a day," remembered Craig.

"Oh, but she's a scout. Scouts are expected to cover even more territory. But for an average grubber, it's quite a walk."

"They don't have to walk so far," said Craig slowly. He was beginning to get another idea. "They could just stay there. If we could only get them up there to the City, and tempt them inside, they wouldn't want to go back. The reason why they didn't try to escape before was because they were too busy. But if the City put them to work, they'd be too busy to come back here."

"Of course they'd come back here," scoffed Cricket. "They'd keep remembering the babies. And babies have to be protected."

"I know," frowned Craig. "We've got to get the babies. Well, how would it be if the soldiers kept the grubbers captive when they arrived? And pretty soon, they'd all be captive, and the nurses would have to go out for food. Then we'd get the babies all right."

"It isn't likely that they would bring eggs and larvae with them when they were hunting for food," Cricket reminded him. "The babies would be left behind in the Cinnamon City.

And if you captured the nurses, they'd feel that they had broken the law, the way Nosy does. And you know how worthless she's become."

"We'll have to explain things to the nurses," said Craig. "We'll tell them that the grubbing parties won't be back, and that they couldn't possibly find enough food themselves to divide with the babies and the red ants. But if they went back and got the babies and brought them to the City Under the Back Steps, there'd be plenty of food, and their sisters wouldn't be captives any more, and they could all start working again, just as they did here, only they'd be working for themselves. They wouldn't be slaves any more."

"Bravo!" applauded Cricket. Then he asked thoughtfully, "But how are you going to get the grubbers inside the City? You can't just invite them to become captives. They might not accept."

"Nosy's going to have to help with that part," declared Craig. "After all, it's her problem, too. Let's go see if she can think of something."

Nosy was glad to see them. She was growing just a little bored with her self-enforced misery and idleness. It was a noble idea to afflict this punishment upon herself, but unless there was someone to witness her suffering, she had come to the conclusion that it was hardly worth while. Her antennae twitched with excitement as Craig explained his newest plan.

"I'll help," she volunteered. "I'll waylay the grubbing parties and offer to lead them to an even bigger catch. I'll take them straight to the City. Oh, the queen will be so pleased with me! She'll have my crime erased from the record immediately. No one will even remember the time when I broke the law, not after this."

"Can the soldiers keep the grubbers there?" asked Cricket doubtfully.

"We can keep the grubbers quiet with the promise that the

babies are on their way," said Nosy confidently. "You're so clever at planning things, I'm sure that won't take any time at all."

Cricket looked at Craig sharply, but Craig refused to meet those bright black eyes.

"I'll start at once," decided Nosy eagerly. "I must find a grubbing party and send them back for reinforcements. There's no use wasting my valuable time on only a few workers."

With an important flirt of her antennae, she hurried down the side of the molehill, and Cricket looked expectantly at Craig.

"What do you plan to do next?"

"I don't know exactly," admitted Craig. "What do you think we should do?"

"Pull a little dirt over our heads and have a nap," Cricket told him promptly. "The sun's beginning to get uncomfortably warm."

15

Jill sat down on the floor of the nursery, and ignored the reproachful proddings of a couple of nannies as they scurried past on some of their endless important tasks. She was tired, and no matter what happened she had to rest a while.

The days and nights spent in the Cinnamon City seemed to her like years, and she was beginning to wonder if she would ever escape. It wasn't that the black nannies in this nursery were unkind. To their way of thinking, they were very kind and they had done everything they could to make her happy. But happiness, to an ant, meant constant work during every hour of both day and night. The little sleep that Jill had been able to snatch had been brief and was constantly interrupted by solicitous nurses proffering new tasks.

She wondered if Craig was finding it so difficult to get his rest. Since the arrival of the Claviger family in the nursery early that morning, she was no longer worried lest Craig and Cricket had been made prisoners like herself. Mother Claviger was full of news of the two of them—rather disconcerting news, to be sure, all about an excursion into the outside world where poisoners were killing insects right and left. They had been lucky to get safely back into the Cinnamon City, according to Mother Claviger, but they had all made it, where a royal welcome had awaited them. The yellow beetle was a little vague about whether or not this welcome extended to Craig and Cricket, but at least she was sure that they were safe from the poisoners. There was going to be a food shortage, too, but naturally it wouldn't extend to the nursery, and as though in proof of that statement she generously offered Jill a drink of her sweet syrup.

The nurses were delighted with the arrival of the sixteen Clavigers for their own especial use. Babies thrived best on milk, and while they could assimilate other juices, the loss of the cows was especially serious to the nursery. But now they didn't have to worry about that. From time to time, grubbers hauled a tasty bit of meat or fungus to the nursery, and then departed. Since the robber ants had not infested these walls, the nurses dined at leisure, feeding the Clavigers, the eggs and larvae as they had always done, and shifting their charges from room to room as the temperature rose or fell. To Jill the life seemed monotonously dull and endless.

Now sharp antennae, which could not be ignored, jabbed accusingly into her shoulder, and she saw that one of the head nurses was standing beside her.

"It's time to carry larvae outside for their nightly airing," reminded the nannie. "Fill your carrying bag and run as fast as you can through the Great Hall. Do not stop to communicate with anyone. There's been some kind of disturbance going on in there all day. We mustn't have the babies upset."

Jill stood up wearily and started toward the rows of soft gourd-shaped larvae. It wouldn't do any good to protest. In the end, she would just have to do as she was told.

As she filled her apron with the little ant babies, she observed that their party to take the air this evening would be larger than usual, for the Claviger family was preparing to accompany the nursemaids. Each of the little beetles was climbing onto the back of a nannie, and since they were of approximately the same size and weight, Jill wondered how the black ants could walk with such a load. Apparently, however, it posed no problem, although all that was visible of the nursemaid was her protruding antennae in front and her six moving legs beneath the yellow Claviger.

There was indeed a disturbance going on in the Great Hall, but the nursemaid on either side hurried Jill along so fast she could not tell what it was all about. The red ants along the walls were opening and closing their jaws with more than their usual vigor, and there seemed to be fewer black workers in attendance tonight. Those who were present were forming a circle in the center of the room, as though they might be preparing to hold a conference, and one of them halted the head nursemaid to touch antennae briefly as she went by.

Jill was far more concerned with seeing whether Craig and Cricket were still here than with the problem confronting the Cinnamon City. She turned her head this way and that, but there was no boy or black cricket to be seen. She hoped, if they had gone back outside, that they wouldn't get in the way of that poisoner.

The area utilized by the Cinnamon City to air its larvae was slightly removed from the main entrance, and partially concealed by the drooping leaves of a low branch of the hydrangea. The nurses placed their small charges on the ground, all but Jill giving them affectionate licks as they did so. She unloaded the contents of her apron, which by now was growing decidedly soiled, and settled herself next to the larvae for a nap, since this was one of the few times when she was permitted to do so. But tonight, even before she could close her eyes, the head nurse was beside her.

"You must stay awake," ordered the nannie. "The responsibility is upon your shoulders this evening."

"What responsibility?"

"The responsibility of guarding the babies," answered the nurse. "It is most unprecedented, but an emergency has arisen in the Cinnamon City. Every black ant must attend a council. It will be brief, of course, for we dare not leave the larvae untended very long. You and the dear Clavigers must watch them for us until we return."

"But the Clavigers haven't any eyes," protested Jill. "They can't watch. And what would I do if something comes along and threatens them?"

"Wave your carrying bag," advised the nurse. "It's such an odd thing that it's sure to frighten enemies. They'll never have seen anything like it, and by the time they recover from their fright, we will be back. It was inconsiderate of our sisters to call this meeting at a time when the larvae were outside the nursery, but it's done now and can't be helped."

With a professional twitch of her antennae she was gone, taking the other nurses with her. Jill sighed, but obediently got to her feet.

"I must say, this is such a joke," said Mother Claviger, stumbling toward her blindly. "I laughed to myself about it every time they used to bring me up for an airing, but of course I couldn't say anything then. It wouldn't have been safe."

"What was a joke?" asked Jill.

"Why right here is the place where I hid my eggs," confessed Mother Claviger. "My fifteen beautiful children were hatched underground where we are now standing. Oh, what those nurses wouldn't have given for a bite of them then, but they were much too busy tending their own children to think that there might be a fat little grub only a few inches away. And now, of course, it's too late."

"How can you be sure this is the same spot?" wondered Jill.

"I should think one piece of ground would feel a lot like another."

"Not at all," objected Claviger quickly. "There's a great difference. Oh, I may not have eyes, but I have no trouble finding my way around. Here is where I hid my babies. Over there is the main entrance to the Cinnamon City. And just out there, a little way, is that mountain where your friends Craig and Cricket make their headquarters."

"Are you sure?" In her excitement, Jill grabbed the yellow beetle by the end of her long nose.

"Of course I'm sure," said Claviger, shaking loose indignantly. "Do you want me to prove it?"

"Oh, yes," cried Jill. "Yes."

Claviger started off at once, and Jill followed. All thoughts of the helpless larvae lying there under the hydrangea leaves had vanished from her mind. She had suddenly realized that she was free. There was no black ant to pull her back and bid her go to work. And right ahead, if Claviger was telling the truth, were her cousin Craig and their friend Cricket. Now they could return together to the City Under the Back Steps, and perhaps the queen would be in a compassionate mood and return them to their normal size.

Suddenly her ears were filled with a whirring sound. A rush of wind blew her hair and skirt, and a huge black shape nearly brushed her to the ground as it settled down beside her.

"Hello, hello, Jill Dear," cried Cricket joyfully. "From the mountaintop we saw you coming, Cousin Craig and I, and we both came to meet you."

"Are you all right, Jill?" called Craig, as he slid down Cricket's slippery side. "How'd you ever get out alone?"

To her own surprise, Jill found she couldn't answer. Perhaps it was because she was so very tired, but tears filled her eyes, then slid down her cheeks, and the first thing she knew she was crying so hard she couldn't stop. Cricket gathered her comfortingly in his two front legs, reaching around to pat her with one of his back ones.

"Jill Dear seems to be losing some of her juices," he told Craig.

"She's crying," explained Craig. "It's because she's a girl. But I'd still like to know how she got out of there alone. Did you bring her, Claviger?"

"I was leading her to your mountain," said Claviger proudly. "But I didn't bring her outside. The black ants brought us both for our nightly airing. My dear children are here, too."

"But where are the black ants now?"

"They've gone to attend a council," Claviger told him. "I think it's about the food shortage. You two were quite right. I heard some of the discussions. It's hurting the Cinnamon City, although, of course, it won't affect us in the nursery. It seems that several of the grubbing parties which went out during the day haven't returned as yet."

"They won't, either," Craig assured her with satisfaction.

"You mean they, too, have been poisoned?" demanded the yellow beetle in alarm.

"No. They've gone to the City Under the Back Steps. And they'll stay there, too," said Craig, crossing his fingers and hoping that there were enough black soldiers to keep the captive grubbers under control. "You see, things are a lot better over there. They're used to things happening to their cows, so they always keep some underground. And there's a garbage can near the back steps, and sometimes the lid isn't on too tight."

"Is that so?" Claviger was impressed.

"And there's no red ants there," continued Craig, remembering that the yellow beetle had once admitted that she wasn't too fond of the rulers of the Cinnamon City. "Nothing but nice black ones. Things are going to get worse and worse here. There won't be any food at all when the grubbers don't come back."

"Some of the grubbers are bound to get back," insisted Claviger. "They'll send out more and more. Even some of the nannies will become grubbers, if things get bad. It's possible that's the reason for the council going on right now. Perhaps they're preparing to send some of the nannies out after food."

"Then they won't come back, either," claimed Craig. "They'll stay where there's plenty to eat."

"If things are going to be as bad as you say, perhaps my children and I ought to change our residence," worried Claviger. "I'm sure we would be welcome. They'll love our sweet syrup, once they taste it."

"I'm sure they will," agreed Craig. Then before Claviger could change her mind, he turned to Cricket. "Would you fly the Clavigers over to the back steps? And Jill, too? I think she ought to get out of here."

Jill had been listening to most of the conversation between Craig and Claviger. When she heard her cousin's airy explanation that her tears were because she was a girl, she had managed somehow to get herself under control. She couldn't understand why Craig was so sure the grubbing parties would not return to the Cinnamon City, but it was very easy to see that he wanted the Claviger family to leave. She herself, however, had no intention of being separated once more from her cousin. If she returned to the City Under the Back Steps, why didn't he?

"I suppose I can fly them over," admitted Cricket ungraciously. "But for the first time in my life, I sympathize with those animals who play host to lice and fleas."

"Why aren't you coming?" demanded Jill, looking at Craig. "Cricket won't mind carrying one more."

"Because I've got to stay and see the nurses," explained Craig. "I've got to talk them into going back after all the eggs and larvae and pupae. If we can only return the babies, the queen's promised to change us back the way we should be."

Then he went on to tell her what had happened, all about Jim spraying the old rosebush and killing the green cows, about bringing the robber ants to the Cinnamon City, and about how the grubbing parties were being waylaid and held captive.

"They wouldn't escape by themselves," he concluded, "so we have to force them into it. They'll be very happy once they get there. They don't even realize what it's like to be free."

"Of course not, the poor things," said Jill sympathetically. "Well, the larvae are right here. Why can't Cricket return them with the Clavigers? Only we'd better hurry before the nannies get back from their meeting."

They had forgotten about the return of the nurses, and now they raced back to the hydrangea bush as fast as they could. Mother Claviger began making the rounds of her children, explaining about their move, and helping each one to climb up on Cricket's steep back. Craig and Jill approached the long rows of larvae.

"There's so many," said Craig doubtfully. "And how are they ever going to hang on? They haven't any feet."

"There's not so many as you think," Jill assured him. She untied her pinafore, spread it on the ground, and began picking up larvae, one at a time, looking at each one carefully. Some she replaced on the ground, others went in the skirt of her pinafore. "Some of these are red ant larvae. You don't want to take them, do you? I think we can get all the black ones in my apron, and tie up the sides so they won't fall out. Maybe Cricket could carry the strings in his mouth."

"You can carry it yourself," suggested Craig.

"Oh, no," she told him firmly. "I'm going to stay here. You'll need me when you talk to the nannies."

By the time the sixteen Clavigers were loaded onto Cricket's back, Jill had finished sorting the red from the black larvae. She folded in the ends of her pinafore, wrapping the strings around to hold it fast, and when she had tied a knot there was just enough material for Cricket to seize in his mouth. As he rose in the air, the dangling bundle swayed gently, and reminded the children of soiled washing, all done up in a sheet, waiting to be collected by the laundry.

"I hope they won't have any trouble," worried Jill. "And that they get there all right."

"They'll get there," Craig assured her confidently. "Only you should have gone with them."

"Oh, no. The nannies know me. They don't know you."

As she spoke the first nursemaid inched herself out of the tiny hole in the ground. She was followed immediately by a line of her sisters, who ran immediately to the red ant larvae, licking and turning each one. At first the children thought that they did not realize the loss of the black ant babies, but in just a few moments the head nurse left the others and came to stand in front of them.

"These are not all the larvae which were left in your charge." Her three white eyes stared accusingly at Jill, and her antennae trembled with agitation. "And our dear Clavigers are missing, too. Where are they?"

She had ignored Craig, but he put out his hand boldly.

"The Clavigers have gone to your true home, the City Under the Back Steps," he told her. "And they've taken all the black ant larvae with them. The only way you can ever see them again is to go there yourself and take all the eggs and pupae with you."

"This is my home. I can remember no other." The white eyes turned to him for a moment, but it was obvious that she preferred to communicate with Jill, for she kept her antennae on the girl's forehead. "Why did you let them go?"

"The babies will be taken care of," Jill assured her quickly. "They came from the City Under the Back Steps, and they're being returned there. That's where you came from, too. And it's where you belong."

"I belong in the nursery," the nannie reminded her. "We still have eggs and pupae there. I must return and care for them."

"You must go and get them. Bring them here," Jill corrected. "We're going to take you all back to your home where you won't be slaves any longer. You'll be free."

"And hurry," urged Craig. "Your sisters who went out for food earlier today are already there waiting for you. They won't come back."

"They would never leave us without food," protested the nurse.

"They can't really help themselves," explained Craig. "You see, they're being held prisoners. They won't be allowed to come back until all the eggs and larvae and pupae that were stolen the other day are returned."

"The red warriors will go after them," said the nurse. "And they'll bring back the larvae as well."

"The red ants are getting weak from hunger," Jill reminded her. "You know they have to eat all the time to keep up their strength, and the grubbing parties aren't bringing any food. We've been lucky in the nursery, but it's been pretty bad in the rest of the Cinnamon City today."

"It will get worse, too," claimed Craig. "The only way you can save yourselves and the babies is to take them to the City Under the Back Steps."

"Why do you do this thing to us?" demanded the nurse piteously. "Why do you force us to become lawbreakers? When you keep us from eating, you prevent us from taking care of the babies."

"But don't you see? You don't have to be lawbreakers," cried Craig triumphantly. "The black ants want their babies returned. They've got the larvae now. All you and the other nannies have to do is bring the eggs and pupae. You'll be welcome, too, and you'll like it there. It's just like the Cinnamon City, only it's nicer, because you'll be free ants, working for yourselves. The grubbers will be freed, too, as soon as you get there with the babies. None of you will be prisoners."

"And there's lots of work," promised Jill. "Every bit as much as there is here."

"You mean, we will all be our own mistresses?" asked the nurse slowly.

"Of course you will," Jill assured her. "And there's a lovely nursery to work in. And lots and lots of babies to take care of. The only difference is there's no red ants, and the city smells of vanilla, not cinnamon. And you'll be free."

"We will be free," repeated the nurse. It was almost as though she had trouble understanding the meaning of the word. "We must bring the eggs and pupae from the nursery of this city to the nursery of the other, and then we will all be free. Our sisters who are now held captive there will be free, too?"

"Every one."

"I understand," said the nurse after a moment. "We must go below for another council."

She left them abruptly, and they could see that she must be communicating some of their conversation with the other nannies, for she went from one to another, touching each with her antennae. After this they carefully picked up the red ant larvae and all disappeared into the hole under the bough.

The council in the Cinnamon City occupied some time. Cricket returned long before the nurses, and he carried Jill's pinafore, wadded up with the knots still intact, in his mouth.

"Nannie thought you should have it," he told her. "She was surprised that you could manage so long without part of your skin, and she told me to fly back as quickly as I could with it."

"Nannie? My Nannie?" cried Jill joyfully. "I didn't see her after the raid, and I was afraid she'd been killed by the red ants."

"Dear me, no," said Cricket. "She took charge of all the larvae, once the engineers had managed to get them out of your carrying bag."

"Were they glad to see the larvae?" asked Craig. "And the Clavigers?"

"Delighted," said Cricket. "Although at first I had a little trouble convincing the guards that the Clavigers would be useful pets. They'd never seen beetles that gave milk any more than I had."

"You mean, you had to take them clear down into the City?"

"Goodness, no. There are guards at the outside entrance now. You'd never recognize the City. After the last raid, Her Majesty realized the army wasn't large enough, so she's taken steps. All road work and construction is temporarily stopped, and the engineers have joined the army. That's until the next lot of eggs are hatched, of course. They're all going to be soldiers. The queen doesn't intend to take any more chances."

"And did you see Nosy?"

"Certainly. She's having great fun, bringing in one grubbing party from the Cinnamon City after another. But I must say, she was greatly relieved to see the larvae. She hopes it won't be long till you send the eggs and pupae."

"I hope so, too," sighed Jill.

It was almost morning when the nurses began issuing from the hole under the hydrangea. They came in a long line, and each one carefully carried an egg or a pupa in her mouth. Their antennae stood stiffly erect, for communication was unnecessary. The fact that they were there, and that they had brought the captive babies was answer enough to the decision of the council.

"I wish Nosy was here to lead us through the grass," frowned Craig.

"Don't you know the way?" asked Jill in alarm.

"Oh, I can find it," Craig told her. "It takes a little longer, but if we follow along the fence, and turn when we get to the end of the petunias, we'll get there."

"I'll walk, too," decided Cricket. "At least part of the way. My wings are tired."

The three of them headed the procession, and because of a night wind which had sprung up to cool the air, the ants were content to follow at a slower pace than usual. They trotted silently through the darkness, and when Jill turned her head to look over her shoulder, all she could see was the glimmer of white eyes bouncing along, like many golf balls. The ants were always quiet, but tonight she had the impression that they were particularly subdued, which seemed to her very strange. They should be jumping up and down because they were released from their servitude. When they reached the City Under the Back Steps, they would be free citizens, and no longer working for their red rulers.

Then she reminded herself that these ants did not know the meaning of freedom. Their whole world was about to be changed, and perhaps they were wondering what would happen to the red warriors who were left behind. Jill caught her breath at the thought. It was the first time she had remembered them, all the grown warriors, and the red queen and the red babies left behind in the royal nursery. What would happen to them now? They couldn't take care of themselves. They had to be fed and bathed; their city had to be kept tidied up by others; they couldn't gather their own food. Without the black ants, they would die. She turned and grasped Craig's arm impulsively.

"Craig! We've taken away all the workers from the Cinnamon City. The red ants can't live without them."

"Then I guess the City Under the Back Steps won't be bothered by any more raids," said Craig, but he spoke so loudly and roughly that she knew that the fate of the red warriors had also occurred to him.

"The red ants aren't very nice," she said, trying to soothe

her conscience with this thought. "But I don't like to think about anyone starving."

"Oh, if they get hungry enough, they'll have to find their own food," insisted Craig. "They've never had to before. But they say you can do almost anything if you have to."

"I guess so," agreed Jill reluctantly.

Long before they reached the end of the petunias, Cricket grew tired of walking, and volunteered to go ahead and advise the black ants of their approach.

"And let us hope they have the good manners to welcome us with a suitable banquet," he concluded, as he prepared to take to the air.

"Tell the queen to meet us at the front door," called Craig. "She can't change us back again while we're inside the City. And we expect her to keep her promise right away."

"Won't it be wonderful to be us again?" asked Jill, and added wistfully, "As soon as I've seen everybody at home, I'm going to get into my own bed and sleep and sleep and sleep."

The sun was slipping over the horizon before they reached the turn of the flower bed and began cutting across the narrow strip of lawn. It was Jill's first experience with dew, and her teeth were chattering when they finally arrived at the back walk. Now she could see the long line of black nannies perfectly. They followed docilely behind, carrying the eggs and pupae, occasionally flicking off a drop of dew with an antenna. But they still didn't seem excited. Well, what could you expect? Jill asked herself. They didn't know what was ahead of them. But in time they would forget the fate of their former rulers, and then they'd really enjoy life. Jill was beginning to be reconciled to the death of the red ants. After all, they were plunderers and raiders and kidnapers. They killed without pity, and the world could get along much better without them.

As they approached the back steps she squinted her eyes, wondering if someone had emptied the contents of an ink bottle

on the ground. Instead of brown earth, she could see only a great black mass, but as they drew nearer she saw that the blackness was made up of ants. It looked as though every resident of the City had gathered above ground at the entrance to welcome them.

A moment later, two small ants darted away from the others and rushed to meet them. Nosy attached herself to Craig, and Jill found herself being patted and caressed by Nannie's antennae.

"My dear, my dear," exclaimed Nannie affectionately. "I was afraid I would never see you again. I was knocked down in the tunnel and trampled on, and for some time I lay there quite senseless. When I came to, you were gone."

"I was taken prisoner," explained Jill.

"I know. I know. When Cricket came with your carrying bag, I knew you were alive. I was so glad you hadn't broken the law and allowed yourself to be eaten."

"We've brought back all your babies. Those who were stolen last time, and the other times, too. Of course some of them have grown up now, but they used to be your babies," explained Jill. "I hope you're glad to see them."

"Oh, very glad," agreed Nannie heartily. "I hope they'll be happy with us. Some of our other sisters are here, but they seem a little restless."

"It's because they were worried about the eggs and pupae," said Jill wisely. "You know you'd worry about that yourself, Nannie."

"Of course I would," agreed Nannie. "It's the law, and no doubt you're right. And now you must excuse me. I must count the babies and make sure every one has been returned."

She bustled away, and Jill walked over to stand with Craig and Cricket.

"There's a welcoming banquet below," Cricket informed her quickly. "I hope you'll stay to enjoy it."

"We can't," Craig spoke up before Jill had a chance to reply. "Nosy's gone for the queen. If all the babies are here, she'll change us back right away."

"I gave them the message that you were coming," said Cricket huffily, "but Her Majesty refused to leave her apartment until you had actually arrived. She said she was too busy laying eggs to waste any time."

"I shouldn't think she'd worry about more eggs right now," laughed Jill, glancing around. "With all these extra ants they're going to have to make the City bigger as it is."

There were indeed a vast number of ants present, and for once the majority did not seem to be concerned with work. Nursemaids from the City Under the Back Steps had relieved the newcomers of the eggs and pupae they carried, immediately scurrying with them underground, but those workers who remained were rushing around greeting and conferring with the recent arrivals and congratulating one another on this great good fortune. They brushed one another with the combs in their front legs, bestowed affectionate licks, and tenderly touched vanilla-scented antennae. The grubbers from the Cinnamon City were there, too, welcoming the nurses, and introducing them to the residents of the City Under the Back Steps, and the nurses had completely recovered from their former despondency and were having as much fun as any of the others. Jill could never remember having seen a group of people who had seemed to enjoy each other more than these ants.

"I had hoped the ones who live here would make the others feel at home," she confessed to Cricket. "And it does look as though they are."

"Why shouldn't they?" wondered Cricket. "After all, they're sisters. There isn't any real difference."

But there must have been a difference. For as though at a signal, the ants left off greeting one another and divided themselves into two groups. One group remained by the steps; the second, which was composed of all the black workers from the Cinnamon City, collected on the sidewalk. For a moment they eddied on the concrete, a shifting pool of black bodies; then, led by one of their scouts, they struck off in a single line through one of the trails between the grasses. None looked back at their watchful sisters by the back steps, and none lingered behind, and after a few moments, the last one had disappeared from sight.

"Where are they going?" cried Craig. "What happened?"

Jill couldn't answer. She could only stare blankly at the waving grass across the walk, and wonder. Had the black workers from the Cinnamon City forgotten something and returned for it? Had they, perhaps, returned to revenge themselves upon their former captors? Certainly they had been made welcome in their true home. What had made them leave it so soon?

At that moment, Nosy came hurrying up with the news that the black queen had left off laying eggs and was on her way up the tunnel.

"I hope you realize that this is a great concession on the part of Her Majesty," Nosy reminded them severely. "Never before has a queen left her chamber to come to the outside world once she has completed her marriage flight."

Jill interrupted. She couldn't go back to being herself without knowing why the slaves had returned to the Cinnamon City.

"Nosy, why did the black ants leave?"

"Oh, did they leave?" asked Nosy carelessly. "I thought they would."

"But what are they going to do? Where are they going?"

"Why, they're going home, of course. To their home. The Cinnamon City."

"But this is their home," insisted Craig. "They came from here. And you wanted them to stay, didn't you? You were glad to see them."

"Of course we were," agreed Nosy. "Our communication was very pleasant. They would have been welcome to stay had they wanted to. But they never do."

"But why?" insisted Craig. "They were free. Do they like being slaves?"

"Since I've never been a slave ant myself, I don't know the answer to that," said Nosy. "Perhaps they feel it's their duty to go back. Perhaps it's because they've never known another existence. Perhaps it's something else. That's just the way it is. We can't understand, you and I, because we have never been in their position."

"Well, at least the red ants won't starve," sighed Jill. "I couldn't help worrying about that."

"And you got your babies back," Craig reminded Nosy. "And now we're going home."

"I'll be sorry to see you go," confessed the scout. "I can't imagine why you want to be a Masher."

"I'm afraid I couldn't make you understand that any more than I can understand why the slave ants went back to the Cinnamon City," confessed Craig. His hand fumbled in his pocket, and a moment later he pulled out his Boy Scout knife. "Here, Nosy. I want you to keep this to remember me by. It may be a little hard for you to learn how to get it open, but I think you can if you practice."

"Of course I can," said Nosy eagerly. "If a Masher can do it, so can an ant. Thank you. I'll treasure your gift always."

"I'll be sorry to see you go, too," said Cricket mournfully. "I'll miss you both."

Jill threw her arms around Cricket's slippery sides.

"We'll miss you, too, Cricket. And we won't forget you, either. I'll leave little pieces of candy and cake here at the side of the back steps for you and the ants."

"And I'll come out in the evenings and make delightful music for you," promised Cricket. "We'll still be friends, Jill Dear and Cousin Craig, as long as we live."

A messenger ant hurried up to them importantly.

"Her Majesty's party has arrived at the entrance to the City. The Mashers are to present themselves with no loss of time."

"I'll go with you," said Nosy, grasping Craig's arm with one of her front legs.

"Me, too," sniffed Cricket, patting Jill. "I'll be with you till the very end."

Led by the messenger, they started toward the steps, and the crowd of ants fell back to let them through. Suddenly Nannie was there, halting their progress momentarily, her antennae caressing Jill for the last time.

"Goodbye. Goodbye," she said. "I'll never see you again, but I'll never forget that you returned all our babies. We'll miss you in the nursery, and I'll think of you and your carrying bag every evening when we take the little dears out for their airing."

"Oh, Nannie," cried Jill, hugging her quickly. "I'll never forget you, either." A minute later she had untied the strings of her pinafore and slipped out of it.

"This is for you," she said. "You can carry the babies in it, or wrap them up and keep them warm, or whatever you want to do with it."

"You mustn't keep Her Majesty waiting, or she will return to her own chamber," warned the messenger.

Craig grasped Jill's arm, pulling her away from Nannie, who stood there waving her antennae, the small, soiled pinafore draped over one front leg.

My Lady stood guard at the entrance to the City Under the Back Steps, her three milky eyes regarding them haughtily.

"Her Serene Highness has instructed me to say that she is very well pleased with your behavior." My Lady's regal antennae touched them each in turn. "She deigns to accept the Claviger family as a gift to the City, and is gratified at the return of her royal children."

"And she's going——" began Craig, but stopped as Jill stepped hastily on his toe. Craig and My Lady never could get along. He'd just have to keep still and let her do the talking.

"We are pleased to have been of service to Her Majesty," said Jill.

My Lady regarded her with approval. It was evident that she considered a humble attitude correct in approaching the queen of the ants.

"Her Majesty has graciously consented to reward you," she admitted. "It has come to her attention that you desire to return to your former ungainly size."

"Oh, yes, My Lady. Please," Jill told her quickly.

"All workers out of the way!" warned My Lady, flourishing her antennae. And although Jill did not turn to see what was going on, she sensed, rather than heard, a great stir behind her.

"You will now kneel down and extend one of your front feet through the doorway of the City," ordered My Lady, when there seemed to be an end to the confusion.

Craig and Jill knelt on the rough ground and silently extended an arm each into the entrance way under the last board of the bottom step. It was impossible to see anything in the darkness within, but someone must have been there, for Jill heard Craig say "Ouch," and saw him withdraw his arm. A moment later she felt a sharp prick on one of her fingers, and involuntarily she pulled back her own arm.

For a moment nothing happened. They knelt there staring at each other, under the superior white eyes of My Lady, and then Jill felt herself beginning to get a little dizzy. At the same time she seemed to be expanding, for she could feel her skin stretching. The world whirled around, the way it did after she'd twisted the rope in her swing as tightly as it would go and then let it unwind, carrying her with it.

Slowly the whirling world came to a stop. The side of the step stood still and became solid painted boards, and she was looking at the third step, not the bottom one. Above its rise she could see into the yard beyond. She looked down, and from where she was kneeling, it was two feet to the ground, not a fraction of an inch, and My Lady, who a few moments before had been standing at a level so that Jill could look into her eyes, was only a black dot which scurried under a small crack below the bottom step.

They stood up, tall and straight, to look out over the back yard, which didn't appear so very large any more, to the hydrangea bush at the far side.

"That's funny," muttered Craig. "It can't have taken us that long to get from the Cinnamon City to the back steps, can it?"

"How long?" asked Jill absently. It was so nice to be her own size once more, and to be able to see things as they really were. A robin hopped across the lawn, and it was only a little bird, not a ferocious feathered monster.

"All day, that's how long," said Craig in a puzzled tone. "We left there before daybreak, and the sun ought to be shining on that bush right now. Instead of that, it's all shadowy, like it gets in the late afternoon."

"What difference does it make?" said Jill impatiently. "So long as we're home. Come on."

But before she stepped out of the flower bed, she looked down, fearful lest she might step on one of her friends or acquaintances from the City Under the Back Steps. Sure enough, there, on the ground close to her foot, was a scurrying little ant, bearing in her jaws a white object larger than herself. As Jill watched, the insect patiently climbed up the side of a smallish dirt clod, then scampered down the other side before disappearing under the crack of the bottom board. She was followed a moment later by a second ant, also carrying a white object, and Jill involuntarily glanced toward the walk from which they had both come. What she saw made her grasp her cousin's arm in amazement.

"Craig!" she gasped. "My cookie crumbs! Look, they're still on the walk."

"Don't be silly," said Craig, but his voice sounded a little uneasy. "Cricket ate the last of those a long time ago. Somebody else has dropped some crumbs."

"I guess so," agreed Jill, but she couldn't help feeling a little uneasy herself. She looked beyond the little pile of crumbs to the place where the winged ants had fallen. There had been many of them earlier, but now the walk was clean and bare. If only she had asked Nannie what finally happened to the lifeless bodies of the princes after the marriage flight, but she hadn't thought to do so. Perhaps, by this time, they had been neatly gathered up by the City undertakers and buried in the ant cemetery. Nannie would have known about it, and told her if only she'd asked. Now she tried to remember Nannie herself, exactly how she looked, and how it felt when those sharp little antennae rapped against her head, but somehow the picture wouldn't come out straight in her mind.

"It couldn't have been a dream," said Craig, as though he might have been reading her mind. "We couldn't both have had the same dream at the same time. And besides, we weren't asleep. But it is funny about those shadows. They were nearly like that when I came around the house and found you sitting here feeding cookies to the ants."

"Of course it wasn't a dream," agreed Jill, but now that she considered it, the whole experience was becoming more like one every minute. Parts of it were fading in her mind so fast that she had trouble remembering them at all.

"But there's one thing sure," said Craig, frowning at her. "Nobody'll ever believe us if we try to tell them what happened. You know how people are when you tell them things they don't want to believe."

"I know," agreed Jill fervently. "But what will we say if they ask us where we've been? And they're sure to ask."

"Maybe they won't," insisted Craig. "Maybe they'll ask us something else instead, something like"—his face grew very thoughtful, and she could see him fumbling in his pocket—"like how I happened to lose my new Boy Scout knife. I had it, just a little while ago. Maybe it slipped down one of the cracks in the steps."

"And my pinafore!" cried Jill in alarm. "I'm sure—at least I'm almost sure I wore it today. But I don't have it on any more. Maybe it was yesterday I wore my pinafore."

"Oh, who cares, anyway?" decided Craig recklessly. "I want to see my folks."

"Me, too," yelled Jill. "Mother! Mother!"

Together they raced up the back steps.

714

210

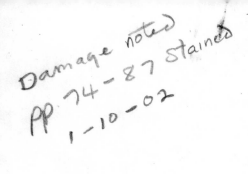

Damage noted
PP. 74 - 87 Stained
1 - 10 - 02